Natural Magick

Aaron's Kiss Series Book 3

By

Kathi S. Barton

WCP

World Castle Publishing
Pensacola, Florida

Copyright © Kathi S. Barton 2011
ISBN: 9781937593612

First Edition World Castle Publishing November 1, 2011
http://www.worldcastlepublishing.com

Licensing Notes

Cover: Karen Fuller
Editor: Brieanna Robertson

DEDICATION

To all the nerds in my life, this means you Paul. I want to thank you for your help with this one. Sometimes you were a little too "helpful", over my head I mean, but you kept the systems straight and the computer online. I love you son. Thanks so much, Mom. Also to all of those who just love a good steamy romance. Thanks to everyone. I hope that you enjoy this third book in the series of Aaron's Kiss and stay tuned for the rest of them. This story is one of my favorites and I hope you love it as much as I do. Kathi

CHAPTER ONE

"Mr. Bartholomew, what did you think you were doing when you did this? You've been caught tampering with the alarm and security system for Mackey Corporation, twice. As much as I hate to tell you this, they are willing to drop the charges if you show them how you managed to circumvent their very expensive system in — it says here in less than fifteen minutes. Is this right?" He turned to his bailiff to confirm the time. It was apparent that the judge was not amused. It was said that he hated hackers and hated young smart-assed ones more. And this company wanting the help of a criminal was not the way the law worked, in his exalted opinion.

"That's not correct, sir. My client is a female."

The public defender had had it pointed out to him just this morning, and was unthinkingly glad to have someone else make the same mistake. As soon as he heard the woman next to him snicker, he knew he had made a tactical error.

"You really think that this is the time or the place to point out that instead of a boy, your client is a girl? What possible reason could I care what his or her gender is? We are here because that person standing next to you hacked into a company's system and tampered with it. A company, I would like to point out to you, that she does not work for."

Judge Lucas was known for his short fuse and his even shorter temper when it came to hackers. And it was just their luck that they drew him today of all days. Pete said nothing as she stood there with her court appointed lawyer.

"No, sir, I don't. I apologize for that. My client is willing to work with the company and show them what she was able to do."

The judge glared. Pete Bartholomew smirked. It was fine by both, it appeared, that there was no love lost between them.

"Fine! Case dismissed. You have five days to comply with the company's request. Next case. And you." He jabbed the gavel toward Pete. "Get out of my court room."

~~~

"When can you come by and show us your work?" Jacob Sailor wanted to get this over with as soon as possible. He was waiting outside the court room for Pete when she exited. He was the one who had recommended the security firm that had been hacked into by this twit, his brother-in-law's firm, to be perfectly honest.

"I can be there now, or in the morning after eleven. I have another job until ten and can't be there until then." Pete answered him with a smirk.

"Another hack job you have to correct?"

Jacob was royally pissed. He didn't want to be here, not with her and certainly not in this courthouse. It gave him the creeps for some unknown reason. His boss, Mr. Mackey, had not been happy about how easily the new system had been broken it to, and in less than fifteen minutes after it had been demeaned complete and operational. The whole system had taken nearly a year to write and another six months of glitches to work out before it was finally working. Then minutes after it was installed, the entire company's bank records, financial statements, profit and loss, everything was captured. At least she hadn't done anything with the information. She had just emailed the entire package to the president with a little note telling him he had been hacked and how easily it had been done.

"Nah, this one pays. You should really try and curtail your gambling online on the company time there, Mr. Sailor. Its company time you're screwing around with. You're not going to be able to borrow much more against your 401k, and everyone else's."

Jacob stuttered for a few seconds, shocked that she had that information, and that she was also correct. He looked around to see if anyone else heard her then realized that no one would care. He was a well-dressed rich man and she was...well, she wasn't.

"You just mind your own fucking business and I'll mind mine. What I do with my money isn't your concern. You're just lucky no one is putting your ass in jail like I suggested. And be warned that I still have the ear of the president, hack."

"Whatever. Remember, fuck-tard, what goes around can come back and bite that tight ass of yours. So which will it be, now or later? No sweat off my back."

He watched Pete as she looked around the hall, probably looking for a fast trick, he thought. She looked...well, bored came to mind. As if she didn't have a single care in the world. Probably didn't, he thought, living off other people's money she had stolen, no doubt. He stiffened again, remembering her comment. That's not what he was doing at all. He was investing the company money, not stealing it.

"Tomorrow morning, and don't be late. I have a full schedule. I don't want to be waiting on you all day to show up."

Jacob realized he needed away from her before he gave in and simply backhanded her hard across that smart mouth of hers. He might have, too, if he wasn't afraid she'd hit him back. Women like her usually used violence when they were confronted with someone smarter than them. He straightened up, knowing he was the better person for not hitting her when she so richly deserved it.

"No problem. See ya in the morning, Jakey boy."

Before he could correct her on his name, she turned and walked away. Insolent bitch! Well, he would show her in the morning. He would make her wait on him until he was good and ready. Petty? Of course it was, but he was a petty sort of guy.

~~~

Pete was at the office of the Mackey Corporation at ten-thirty the next morning. She hadn't dressed up. Her jeans and baggy flannel were clean; her black high tops were scuffed but laced up tight, and clean as well. She went directly to the reception desk and told the woman the who, what, and when of her visit. Shelia asked her to wait, as Mr. Sailor was in a meeting. She gave Pete a little smile as if to say, "He told me to say that," and then winked.

Forty-five minutes, later Shelia called Mr. Mackey.

"Ms. Bartholomew has been here nearly an hour and Mr. Sailor has yet to come and get her. I don't think he's being very professional." She turned her back to Pete to continue to speak into the phone in lowered tones. "He told me to say that he was in a meeting. I don't think that's where he's at. He called her the 'hacker extraordinaire.' What would you like for me to do?"

Shelia had been with the company for many years, working her way up through the ranks as her father had told her to. "If you want to learn a company from the inside out, then start with the bottom rung of the ladder," he had told her. So she had, and now she sat at the front desk to learn that part of the job, and her daddy, the one and only Mr. Karl Mackey himself, was quite proud of his little girl. And no matter what Pete had done, she had caused the company no harm, but had saved them a great deal of embarrassment if the records had been sent anywhere but to her father. Shelia also believed that Jacob Sailor was an ass.

"Don't let her leave, honey. I'll be right there. If Sailor shows up, well, I want you to keep Ms. Bartholomew there. All right?"

"Of course, Mr. Mackey. You know you can depend on me."

Less than two minutes later, Karl came around the corner to receive the young woman.

"Ms. Bartholomew, I'm Karl Mackey, sorry to have you keep waiting. Come with me, let me show you around. Shelia, when Sailor finally decides to grace us with his presence, please tell him that Ms. Bartholomew is in a real meeting and we are not to be disturbed."

~~~

Karl had asked Sailor what Pete would require to show the tech team what she had done to break into their system, and Sailor had responded that she just needed a computer. It became apparent that Sailor had not bothered to ask or get any information. He had just assumed. Karl was beginning to see that this was the way Sailor did most of the things he had been assigned, half-assed.

"We can get you whatever you need to work with. There are ten techs that want to meet with you, pick your brain so to speak. Let me introduce you to them then let's get you started. I'm sorry; I didn't catch your first name."

"Pete, I go by Pete."

When she looked at his face, almost daring him to make a comment, he left it at that. She had a pair of dark sunglasses on, but Karl knew that she was looking him in the eye. He had a lot of friends who had to wear sunglasses during the day and didn't think anything of her doing so now. He was impressed with Pete already and Karl Mackey was not a man who was easily impressed.

At six o'clock, Karl went to the third floor conference room to see how the meeting had gone. He'd been tied up all day in one meeting after another and hadn't had time to go anytime earlier. He'd just gotten off the elevator when he saw one of his people still at his desk. He told Karl that he'd not seen any of them all day and thought they might be still at it. He believed that they were still in the conference room on the fifth floor. Karl looked at his watch to make sure he had not misread the time as he took the elevator up. It turned out the intern was correct, all of them were still deep in conversation and looked to be nowhere close to wrapping up when he opened the door.

There were large post-it sheets hanging on the walls and doors. Several white boards had been brought in and were covered in, well, he didn't know what the hell it was, but it looked complicated. The ten people who were in charge of his IT lab were frantically taking notes and making adjustments on their laptops. Pete was sitting on one of the long conference tables with her feet in the seat of one of the chairs, throwing a ball up in the air while talking a mile a minute, seemingly oblivious to the fact that they were hanging on her every word. When he cleared his throat, all eyes, including hers, turned to him.

"Good evening. I had thought we'd have wrapped up by now. Have you run into problems?" Karl asked the room in general.

"Oh shit...sorry, Pete, ma'am. Oh, no sir, she showed us the glitch in the system and we fixed those already about..." He glanced down at his watch and looked as amazed as Karl had been when he realized that it was almost six-thirty. "Almost six hours ago. I didn't realize it was so late."

Daniel Scott had been in charge of the security lab for the Mackey Corp for nearly ten years. Karl thought if she could make him, of all people, lose track of time, then he needed to take a closer look at this girl and maybe what she could offer all the holdings in this company.

"Then this would be...?" He encompassed the room with all of the papers and notes lying around.

"She was showing us other glitches, fixable glitches in a few other systems we have running. Payroll, for one, and a couple of the camera programs running the outside security that needed a boost as well."

"Great. That's really...wait, payroll had a glitch? What kind of glitch?" He looked over at Pete with a questioning look.

Pete walked over to one of the computers and pulled up his entire payroll roster in a matter of a few key strokes. He wasn't even sure he could do it that quickly and he had been doing it for years. He thought he might have to take a few lessons himself if she was that good.

"See this? It's your left over decimal. It doesn't really add up to much per check, but over your entire payroll yearly, it's about four million dollars."

"Please tell me that you haven't tapped into that one as well." Karl was suddenly nervous, very nervous. She had been caught hacking into his system and here she was in his payroll now and to the tune of four million dollars. Small cells and bars flashed in his mind.

"I'm not a thief, Mackey. If I wanted to get to your money, I could have taken it days ago, no weeks ago." Pointing to Daniel, Pete continued. "He can show you the rest, and I've showed them how to change the passwords and how often to do it. By the way, Jacob Sailor had his brother-in-law install your security system, right? I tapped into your system to let you know that he isn't using standard procedures and he's a fucking thief. I fixed your payroll, but you may want to check with your accounting department. A lot of money can be moved in two weeks. And your boy Jakey? He has a major gambling problem and is using the company's 401K as his personal bank account." She gathered up her things and started toward the door.

"Ms. Bartholomew, I'm sorry. I was wrong about you, very wrong. It's been a hell of a week and I may have...if you will, I'd like to extend you a permanent job if you'll take it. We could all use someone like you on our side." Karl was humbled. He had insulted the girl and she had still made sure he knew about Sailor and the rest of the inner workings of their flawed system. He didn't run across a lot of honest people in his line of work and even less of people who would help him after he had insulted them.

"It's Pete, and no thanks. I believe I have fulfilled my required services by the law, Mr. Mackey. If there is nothing else, then I'm going home." She didn't turn around when she answered him. But being what he was, he could smell that she was upset, pissed really. And he didn't blame her.

"Ms...Pete, thank you. Yes, of course, you're finished, and you've more than fulfilled the terms of our agreement. I'll be sure to call the judge first thing in the morning and let him know what a valuable asset you were to us today."

CHAPTER TWO

"Yes, I'd like to talk with Peter Bartholomew if you please," he explained when someone finally answered.

Duncan loved the phone. Especially the little cell phone with all its magic. He was the man servant to Aaron and Sara MacManus. He took care of the household for his master long before his mistress had joined them, and would do so for many years to come. He helped in the things that Aaron had been unable to do when he'd first had Duncan join him, and he helped the mistress now in the same capability.

"Yeah, hang on. Gotta go see what's cookin' with her," the voice on the other end of the receiver told him.

Duncan had called the local college just this morning to see if they could send out someone to help with the purchase of several computers. They, in turn, suggested that he call Pete Bartholomew.

His lordship, Aaron, was trying to sort through the paperwork that had been left to him and it was, frankly, not going well. Master Colin, new master vampire in his own realm, was having as much if not more difficulty than his friend Aaron. Neither previous master had taken the time to keep computerized records. Everything had been hand written and if one was lucky enough to be able to read the notes, they were stained and wrinkled and there were no dates or real information to go on.

Calling the college had been the mistress' idea. Sara thought that hiring someone from the university would give the student some extra cash and a little experience as well.

"Pete here."

Duncan, deep in his mussing, was startled by the sharp tone of this voice. The voice itself had surprised him. He didn't know why, but had thought the young man would be much older. With all the compliments he had been given about him, it was hard to imagine this voice matching the image he had in his head.

"Mr. Bartholomew, my name is Duncan and I was told by the university that you could help us purchase a good computer and all the hard…hardware that went with it. I was wondering if you'd be available to do that for us."

"It's just Pete. Who did you speak to at the college?"

Duncan did not blame Pete for asking for more information. There were a lot of sick humans out in the world.

"Oh, yes, a Mr. Sage. An Edward Sage of the college IT department. When I asked for the best, he suggested that I hire you."

He had actually told Duncan that he would be stupid not to hire Pete to help out. Edward said Pete did every install job he or the college ever had. Edward went on to say that Mr. Bartholomew was dependable and honest, as well as cheap.

"Okay, sure. When is great for you? I have a job until ten in the mornings and another job that starts at six. I have stuff to do in between, but if you let me know what day is good for you, I can move stuff around."

Duncan could hear a lot of noise in the background and wondered if he had interrupted a party.

"Tomorrow would be good for me, or today if there is time. I have a very flexible schedule, Mr. Pete, and I will be at your trash. I can either meet you somewhere or you may come here. I have been given permission from the master to see this through."

"It's Pete. It's almost eleven now, so I still have time to do a soft shoe shuffle to get some free time today. How about you meet me at Homer's Electrical? It's on Howard Street. We won't be shopping there, but it's a big place and easy to find. I can be there in fifteen, how about you? And it's disposal, not trash."

"Oh, yes. Disposal. Fifteen? Yes, please, would you wait for just a moment if you please, sir?" Duncan had tried keeping up with her, but the terminology Pete was using was just too much for him. He turned to the mistress who had just walked in and simply handed her the phone with a brief explanation. Sometimes he thought it better just to have someone else translate for him rather than him trying to muddle through.

"Yes, Mr. Bartholomew, my name is Sara MacManus. I can be there in about twenty-five minutes. I'll be coming along with Duncan. We are in need of several computers with printers and things, is that all right?"

"It's Pete, just plain old Pete. Whatever you want. I'll be standing outside the big arrow. I'll have my bike out front of the place. Don't go in. Homer's an ass and will rob you blind in a heartbeat." Then the phone went dead.

~~~

They took a little longer than what they had first thought because Shade had decided to go along with them. Then Mel wanted to have lunch afterwards so the three women and

Duncan piled into the Hummer at eleven fifteen. When they pulled up in front of Homer's, they were about twenty minutes later than planned. The place was as easy to find even from the highway. When they got out of the vehicle and looked around, there was a bike just where Pete had said it would be. Only the bike out front was a large motorcycle, not the bicycle they had assumed would be there.

"I'm so sorry we're late. I hope we haven't put you out any. My name is Sara MacManus this is Shade Larimore, Duncan, and Mel Keeper." Sara put out her hand as she spoke.

Mel had liked the last name that Sara had made up for her when they had had dealings with Shade and Colin's adopted boy, Brent, so they continued to use it when they'd had to deal with anything related to the human world.

Mel, or Queen, Melody, Mistress of Light, Keeper of Magic, as her title dictated, came to the human side of the realms often. Sara loved her to death. She was also her cousin. The two women were good friends. But there were times, like the ride over to the computer place, that Sara wanted to hit her. When Mel and Duncan got together, it was more likely than not enough to drive a person insane.

"Pete Bartholomew. No biggy. I have nothing but time today. You can follow me to the computer store." She walked away from them without taking her hand, settled herself on the Harley, pulled on a dark helmet and waited for them.

"Well, that was just rude, don't you think?"

Mel had learned to curb her tongue around humans now. At least this time she had waited until they were all settled in the car before saying anything, for which Sara was eternally grateful. Mel could be a tad...harsh, she supposed was a kind word.

"I don't think we have any right to be upset with him, especially since we were the ones who made him wait. He did tell us he had to move things around and probably thought we weren't coming after all." Sara settled back into her seat and buckled. "Also, he's blocking us, hard too. I wonder if it's natural or planned. Get anything, Mel?" Sara was the strongest mentalist in the group and if she could not read the young man, then maybe Mel's magic could.

"I didn't even try. That boy could use a little bit of manner training as far as I'm concerned." Sara just rolled her eyes. Like Mel had a lot of room to talk where dealing with people was concerned.

They followed the bike through medium traffic, and Sara was grateful that Pete kept slowing down in deference to Duncan's slow driving. When they got to the store parking lot, everyone got out once again. Pete was already waiting by the bike and when they were all situated, they went inside.

"What are the primary uses for these computers? Who will be using them, and for what propose? Are you going to be surfing, browsing, keeping books, or just wanting a fancy paperweight?"

Sara smiled. She normally did not like a person who was so blunt, but she seriously didn't think this person was being rude so much as it was his nature. But Mel didn't understand the difference, or she just didn't care apparently.

"You know, you're kind of rude," Mel said.

When Pete simply nodded at Mel and told her, "Thanks," it was all Sara could do not to laugh out loud.

"So, what are you gonna do with them? The man I talked to said you needed to have a complete set up. Is that true?"

Most people professed to not caring about how a person felt about them but really did deep down. This young man, Sara thought, really seemed not to care at all.

"I believe we will need two for bookkeeping, for two separate households. The other references I do not understand as I do not have a great deal of experience with computers. Let us assume that we will need them to do everything. With the exception of the paperweight. I believe his lordship has one of those already."

Duncan was not trying to be smart, or funny, but his prim and proper slant on everything was just Duncan's way. Sara waited for a snide comment from the man, and was surprised and glad when none came forth.

"Fine, let's have at it, shall we?"

When they entered the store, they were immediately overwhelmed by the scope of it all. Everywhere they looked was some new gadget to look and play with. It looked as if they were not getting out of there without some major purchases if the other women had anything to say about it, Sara thought.

They were greeted by a sales person named Toby and he had already been told they were coming by Pete, it seemed.

"Pete, long time, no see. Still hacking up the world one PC at a time?" he asked with a huge grin.

"Nah, just trying to secure my million is outta the hands of perverts like you. Toby, this is the group I called you about. Duncan, Ms. MacManus, Ms. Keeper, Ms. Larimore, this is Toby Stark; he owns this place. They need at least two desks, and I think two or three laps."

"May I have a quick word with Pete for a second, please?" Sara pulled the kid over to the corner and looked up into the sunglasses that had not been removed when they came inside. "Will you take off the sunglasses? I'd like to see who I'm talking with." When Pete complied, Sara could only stare.

"Do you need to wear them for protection or something else? Your eyes are quite handsome. I don't believe I've ever seen silver eyes before."

"Both. What did you want? And just for the record, I don't care if you think they're nice or not."

Sara wanted to say more, but held her tongue, for now, at least. "I believe as you can tell, we know squat about computers, but if you think by bringing us to your friend and soaking us for a lot of money is going to work then you're barking up the wrong bush."

"It's tree, not bush, and for the second time this week, I'm not a thief. Toby is a friend of mine, yes. When I can I steer business his way, I do it. When someone tells me that they want to best, he is also the man I go to. If you'd rather go elsewhere, fine with me. There isn't a computer store around the state that doesn't know who I am. I'm helping you shop on my own time, Mrs. MacManus. I could care less if you like me or not. If it's a matter of you trusting me, then that's okay too. I'm sure there is any number of people who'd be happy to help you."

Sara started to snap back when she looked at Pete. Really looked. Pete had a smooth face, button nose, full, sensual lips, and no Adam's apple. Sara stepped back, shocked. "Oh my God, you're a woman! I assumed...well, we all assumed really, what with the butch clothes and bike. And what's with your name?"

Sara immediately felt terrible. She watched as the woman's face flamed with embarrassment as Pete looked around the store to see if anyone had heard what Sara had said. A few of the other customers glanced their direction, but not too many.

"It's none of your business what kind of name it is, it's mine. Now if we could get this friggin' show on the road, I'd really be happy." She hissed at her, turned away, and headed toward the laptops that Toby had on display. Pete had been short and snappy with her, but Sara felt as if she deserved it. She had humiliated the bo...girl, and she felt terrible for it.

~~~

No one had ever reacted that way when they realized their mistake about her gender. Pete never corrected them. It wasn't really such a big deal and she let them assume anything they wanted about her. She did wonder what she would think if she told her that her first name was Piccadilly. Christ, what the hell had her mother been thinking?

Her birth certificate claimed she was Piccadilly Fresno Bartholomew. Her mother had said that Pete had been conceived in a Fresno hotel called the Piccadilly Inn, thus her name. Her brothers, all six of them, had equally ridiculous names. She knew also that unlike her, they loved theirs. She changed hers to "Pete," and hadn't ever told anyone anything different.

She hadn't seen her mother or her brothers for nearly eight years now. Not since she had turned seventeen and left in the middle of the night without a word to any of them. She wasn't even sure if they were still alive. They had all been living in a trailer in a dank park since she could remember, all seven of them living in a two-bedroom, worn out piece of crap. Pete had three older brothers and two younger ones when she had left home, and all of them were the scum of the earth.

They had been on welfare since she could remember, and they had gotten their phone and electricity shut off at least seven or eight times a year due to non-payment. The town's people where they had grown up were merciless, always turning their noses up at them, making fun of their clothes. Pete had had to grow a very tough skin or she would never have made it through high school.

College was out of the question because she didn't have the money to even apply for the grants so she could go for free. Then there were the fees to apply to the college itself. Pete was smart, very smart, actually. Had she applied herself more in high school, she would have gotten a good scholarship to any college she wanted, but being born on the wrong side of the track and the sheets, plus smart, she would not have stood a chance in the world of ivy leaguers.

Her computer skills had come naturally to her. She had made herself a nuisance at Toby's computer store the summer she turned eighteen and he had let her work for him selling computers. He also let her fiddle with the returns, more often than not fixing them. When he offered to pay for her to take a night class a couple of times a week, then she would pay him back, she jumped at the chance. It was not long before she had earned a reputation for being the best at what she did. Toby had started having people call her directly if they needed something major done and she became an independent geek. She never forgot what he had done for her and brought in as much business as she could. But she was also right in that she was not a thief. She brought customers to him, but she didn't receive or take anything more than good service from him when she needed it.

After a few minutes of calming herself down, Pete moved over behind the women who were going nuts over the "pretty" laptops.

"Have you decided what you will need them for? That will determine how much memory, or storage area you'll need. Say, for example, you were using this one in the kitchen, I'd recommend a desk top. They're stationary and do take up a little more room, but they have more bang for your buck. You can surf the web, or search for things, keep track of a budget, plan menus and file all of your favorite recipes on it. Also, you can download movies and programs, plus watch a DVD on it." Pete pointed to the desk tops just behind her.

"The office computers can be either, but again, I'd go with desk for all the same reasons. With a desk, you can also put in more memory and the parts can be replaced cheaper than on a lap. If the lap gets messed up, then replacement is usually the only option. I can tear into a desk and fix most anything for less than a hundred bucks, sometimes a little more, but not much."

Pete went over every option with them, recommending some, nixing others. She always made sure they knew what they were looking at, and the price it would cost to replace it, or add in later.

When Mel wandered over to the game systems with Pete in tow, she showed the woman which ones had better games versus the ones that were backward compatible. She also showed Mel the display unit of one of the larger gaming systems and how to work the controller to it. After thirty minutes of playing against Pete and losing, Mel had been hooked and purchased one. When Pete told her that she could play online with anyone else who had a like system and the game, Mel bullied the others into buying one as well.

Finally, they went up to the checkout lane, where Toby started checking them out. It had been five hours and Pete was exhausted. It had been fun, she thought. The women all seemed to get along and had been friends forever. Duncan was a hoot and she loved talking with him. She wondered several times just how he fit into the dynamics of the household.

"You've been enormously helpful. Thank you. We couldn't have done with without you, Pete. You have to let us pay you something, anything."

Sara was reaching into her purse as she spoke. Oh yeah, Pete thought, I'm a charity case.

~~~

"Ah, no, no thanks, I gotta go. Toby will take care of you, and if you have any problems, he can...he knows how to reach me. See ya." And she dashed out the door, leaving the little group staring open-mouthed at her quick departure. Toby cleared his throat and when he had their attention, he began ringing them up and talking.

"I've known Pete for a while. You aren't gonna find anyone more knowledgeable then her about most anything. She...well, she doesn't have much...faith in people, I guess. She can be a bit caustic at times, and I'd like to tell you she doesn't mean it, but she just doesn't care what anyone thinks of her. People are a little uneasy about her eyes. I noticed you looking at her without them glasses. That's unusual for her. She never takes them off. Anyway, she was right. If you need help, oh I don't know, setting these up, well I sure wouldn't mind giving her a call direct like for you. Now if there isn't anything else, with her employee discount, it comes to seven thousand eight hundred fifty-two dollars and one cent." Shade burst out laughing.

"Just how much discount does she get? And why did you give it to us?" Mel asked.

"I told you, she's a friend, and its twenty percent. I think you'd probably get the same discount at any of the merchants around here, not just in here. She 'helps' out everyone who needs it and some who think they don't. Like I said, she's knowledgeable about most anything, and doesn't mind sharing what she knows or has."

Chapter Three

The phone was being answered as she was walking by it. And when Bug, one of the people who lived in the building, turned and yelled, "Anyone know if Pete's in the house?" for a second, she thought she might have lost an eardrum.

"Christ, Bug, I'm right here. What's wrong with you? Are you stoned again? Give me the friggin' phone. Pete here," she said into the phone.

"Ah, Miss Pete, it is I, Duncan. We were wondering if you could come out to help us set up the equipment?"

"It's just Pete. I can't today. I have two part-timers today, and three tomorrow night. I could come over tomorrow morning to start, but I'd have to bring help with me. I assume you'll need Internet hauled in too, right? Or have they dropped you yet?"

There was silence at the other end. Pete was wondering if she had lost the connection. Just when she was about to say something, Duncan spoke up.

"Miss, could you repeat that for me, please?"

Pete had to smile. The man had a way about him that just made you want to tuck him into your pocket and keep him there. She didn't know why she liked the man, but he did make her want to get to know him.

"Dunc, if you don't understand anything I'm saying to you, just say so. It won't hurt my feelings. I do tend to talk to people like I listen, short and sweet. I'm sorry, okay; let me repeat that in English for you. Have you called your local Internet provider, or would you like for me to do that? It's usually the cable provider that carries your Internet, but not always. I can have them bring the service to your home, which is where they drop the line from the pole in the yard to your house. It's called a drop. I can bring it in the house for you. My doing it will save you a bundle and I've been certified by the company to do this, so you don't have to worry about me fuc...messing it up for you. Okay?"

"Oh yes, that's much better, much better indeed. Yes, you call the necessary people and we would like for you to bring it into the house. As for help, I will need to clear that with the master or the missus of the house. I'll leave a message with...err that Bug person." She could hear the relief in his voice and grinned at that. Poor Dunc.

"Look, I have a cell...a cell phone, but it's a drop n' kick. Just leave a quick message on it. Also, I'll have someone from the cable place drop off some cables and ties. Hang a sec and let me ask for another phone."

"Oh, Miss Pete, wait, a 'drop n' kick' is what, may I inquire?"

"It's a pay as you go phone. I have to buy the time I use. Less hassle that way. I figured you weren't gonna call and ask me for my favorite recipe so you should be all right with it." Pete laid the phone receiver on top of the pay phone and went to search out another phone to use. She figured this was easier than trying to call him back. "Dunc, Booger wants to know where you live so he can come out and drop stuff off for us to use this morning. He's at work now. He works for your cable company, and it won't be any trouble to do that."

Duncan gave her the address, and had to ask, as she knew he would, "Booger, miss?"

"Yeah, it was an unfortunate incident with his nose, too gross to go into. Suffice it to say that he earned the nickname." She shuddered at the memory. She was glad when he did not ask for more details.

Pete rattled off the address to the other phone, and came back several times to ask or relay information to Duncan.

"So if I may, miss, this unfortunate Booger person is going to drop off a roll of cable at the gate sometime this morning. He will only ring the gate bell, but will not enter. I am to leave a message on your drop it and kick it when it arrives. Is that correct?"

"Yeah, Dunc, that's great. Only its drop n' kick not drop it and kick it. You hang with me and we'll get you up with the lingo." She had to laugh. He was trying very hard and he was so proper it was funny to hear him try and loosen up.

"By the way, miss, what is your favorite recipe, if you don't mind my asking?"

She stopped for a second and thought about it. "I don't have one. Actually, I don't think I've ever had a home cooked meal before. My mom wasn't what one would call domestic. If you couldn't pour it out of a can or a box by yourself and eat it, then you were SOL. And since I've left home, I usually eat on the sly, err pick up what I can at a fast food joint. And before you ask, SOL means 'shit outta luck' as in, 'you're on your own, kiddo.'" Even she could hear the bitterness in her own voice.

"I'm sorry, miss. I did not mean to...that must have been terrible for you."

Pete was quiet for a moment or two, then said, "Thanks, Dunc, I appreciate it, but she made me what I am, I guess. Sad but true. I'll see ya tomorrow then."

~~~

At seven-thirty the next morning, Pete was at the house with Eon. Duncan had left word that it would be fine for the extra help. Duncan had introduced them to Daniel Taggert who ran the security system for the house. Aaron had wanted to make sure that one did not interfere with the other and was glad that she had mentioned it, Duncan had said in his message. They set about the house, figuring out where they were to set up each computer station, a desk top in the kitchen, one in the office, and then a whole house wireless system for the game system and a couple of laptops with printers.

Eon was in charge of bring the cable that Booger had dropped down from the pole just off the property up to the house, then Pete would bring it in and wire the house. She started on the kitchen wall installments while Eon worked his magic outside. The wiring and setting up the computer took nearly two hours, then the system set up took another hour, but no one had to sit with that part for it to work. She went to the office next and was wiring in there when a kid came in. He was very quiet and still for a kid, so it took her a couple of minutes to notice him.

"Hello there. Whatcha doing?"

Pete didn't interact much with kids and had never been very comfortable around them. Usually, they got bored with her because she never talked to them any different than she did the adults she knew.

"I'm wiring up the room for the computer system that's being installed in this house. I've been hired by the lady of the house. Who are you?"

"My name is Brent Shell Larimore. Shade and Colin are my new parents, and I stay with Duncan and Sara sometimes. Who are you?" Cheeky little guy, but she had asked him first.

"I'm Pete Bartholomew, at your service." She held out her hand for him, and he took it with a smile and a firm grip.

That was all the encouragement he needed, apparently, and soon he was nearly in her lap trying to see everything she was doing. She didn't care and was very patient with him, telling him everything he wanted to know, letting him hand her the tools she needed from her big tool box. When Eon came in about an hour later, Pete set him up at the kitchen computer to work through all the set up menu's and the plug and play programs. It wasn't hard work, but it was boring. And Eon's attention span was not really all that long anyway.

Daniel came into the kitchen at lunch time to get a sandwich from Duncan and was surprised by how much they had gotten done. Of course, the house still wasn't hot yet, but Pete would do that herself once Eon left. She was very careful who knew the house schematics of the household systems she installed.

"You guys do fast work, but is it good?"

Pete didn't object to his questions. It was pretty standard of the type of questions she got from the heads of security on all the job sites she went on. This guy wasn't bad. She'd had others who followed her every move making sure she didn't mess up their part of the install.

"Pete's the best. Just ask her, she'll tell ya." Eon was a goof-off, but she liked him anyway. She ruffled his hair as she walked past him.

"She'll tell you what?" Sara had waddled into the kitchen at the end of the conversation so wasn't aware they were talking about Pete.

Pete looked at the pregnant woman. She looked exhausted and tired. Pete could tell that she was carrying twins. She had accidently brushed against Sara the first day. Pete avoided any physical contact with people. Touching had consequences that she didn't care for.

"Pete. I was asking Eon about how good they were, and he said that Pete knew she was good, to ask her. I was just going in to ask her when you waddled, I mean walked in with upmost grace." Daniel grinned and Pete laughed.

Duncan had made several sandwiches and was laying them out on the table with drinks and chips when Brent walked in the kitchen. He'd been "helping" Pete all morning and she had only just escaped him not ten minutes ago.

"See, I told you he would make you a sandrich. They're always good too. He puts me lots a mayo on mine, don'tcha, Mr. Duncan? I told Pete to come and have one too, okay? Her belly was thinkin' her throat was cut, I heard it. Can I have some pop, Sara? I did good at school today."

"Yes, of course. Please have a seat, Pete. There is always plenty to go around. Eon, come on before Daniel eats it all himself."

Pete had never eaten at anyone's house before, opting to go out and bring something back for her and whoever was helping her out at the time, which was not often. There was plenty to go around, too. In addition to the "sandriches," there was chips and potato salad, macaroni salad and fat dill pickles. And plenty to drink as well, beer, tea, a variety of soft drinks, and juice.

Pete had a bottle of water, but Eon and Daniel had opted for a beer each. Eon didn't get to do anything with his but put it to his lips before Pete simply cleared her throat and put out her hand. Eon didn't say a word, but set it in her palm and got himself a pop.

The computer and the gaming system were up and running to full capability at around two-thirty, then Eon left "for another gig," he had told Duncan.

Duncan had had to ask, and discovered that the young man had another job and was still in high school, going to night classes to finish his education. The only way he was able to help Pete out for the extra money was he had to promise he would finish high school. She wouldn't have it any other way. It worked out well for both of them. She got an apprentice, and he was getting his education.

~~~

Aaron just happened by his office as Pete was cleaning up and getting ready to finish for the day. He stopped to listen to the conversation between a woman and Brent. He didn't know the woman's voice, but he knew Brent's. The woman was explaining to him something about an eye problem she had. He had missed the first part of the conversation, but assumed that Brent was being his usual self and asking ninety questions. Aaron loved that about him.

"Well, I wear them because people don't care for the color of my eyes. Plus, it's a little painful around bright lights and the sun sometimes."

"Oh, well, people can be just dumb asses sometimes is what Colin says. I believe him 'cause he ain't never lied to me. Shade either. They're life mates, did ya know that?" Brent asked.

He heard a crash and nearly went in, but as neither person seemed concerned, he let it go for now.

"Watch your language, kid. You're too little to cuss yet." Another crash and still no movement from the two in his office. "Nope, never heard of life mates before, but different strokes for different folks, I guess," she answered him.

"How come you don't got a mate? Shade says that everyone needs a mate to love them. I think she just says that 'cause they kiss and stuff all the time. I think that stuff is gross. Don't you?"

Aaron heard the same crashing sound and again, no one made a sound. It was then that he realized it was tools, some tools being banged together on something soft.

"Kissing? Gee, I don't know, buddy. I've never been kissed before, not really. People aren't attracted to people like me, and before you ask, it's because I was born on the wrong side of the sheets, err...I mean tracks. My kind of...person isn't good enough to have life mates. We're more of the...well, long term commitments aren't something I see a lot of and it's doubtful I ever will. Here, put those back into this case like this."

Aaron felt his own mate coming near him. When she was close enough for him to see, he motioned her to come and have a quiet listen with him at the door.

"They've been talking for the past ten minutes. She is very outspoken. I hope Colin and Shade don't care. It could be an eye opener if Brent repeats anything she's told him," Aaron whispered through her mind with a laugh.

"She'd better not be telling him dirty jokes. Colin will murder her. Not to mention Shade."

"No, love, just listen. You'll see what I mean."

Aaron wrapped his arms around her and placed his hands over his children nestled within her womb. They had learned when she was first pregnant how to talk to them, and loved doing it every chance he got.

"You don't have a boyfriend or nothing? I thought Eon was your lover or something," Brent asked her.

This crash was different, he noticed right away, sounding as if a lot of tools had been dropped. But this time onto a hard surface rather than into a bag.

"Sheesh, kid! Where the hell did you hear that? You don't...you're too young...you know, you're not either of those, are you? Okay, kid, look, I'm only gonna tell you this once so you listen up, all right? No, Eon is not my lover. I don't do sex with kids, nor dumb asses, and he's definitely both. Nor do I discuss either my sex life or my lack of sex life with a seven-year-old. Come to think of it, I don't think anyone wants to discuss their sex life, good or bad, with a seven-year-old. You should save those questions for when you're, say, forty or fifty and then only ask this Colin guy or Shade. Sara obviously knows a little about sex too, so any of the people that you are staying with, the adults you're staying with, ask them. Never ever, ever, ever ask Eon about sex, never. Understand? There's no telling what he'd tell you. And I'd hate to have to pay for the amount of therapy you'd need if you were going to seek advice from Eon again. We square? You get it?"

"Yeah, I gots it. Don't talk to Eon about sex. You're not mad, are you? I mean, you act kinda all mad, but you ain't, are you?"

Aaron stiffened, ready to go in and protect Brent if she were to say one thing to upset him. Brent had had enough for one so young, he thought. Brent's own mother had sold him to men for sex so she could buy drugs. Brent's little sister Becca had been murdered for the same reasons. The only thing that kept Aaron from storming in was Sara's hand gripping his.

"Nah, kid, I'm not mad. I don't get mad all that easy. But I suspect I'm gonna be yelled at about this sometime tomorrow though. What do you think, buddy?"

Aaron felt it then, a very gentle probe of magic, a small touch. He also knew that she had been looking to see who was near, much like he had done when Sara was coming up the stairs moments ago. He moved into the room. He wanted to finally meet this woman, this paragon of mystery.

"You should be fine with Colin and Shade, as you were honest with him and gave him good advice, I believe. Thank you," he said. "My name is Aaron. I'm happy to meet you finally."

So he was introduced to Pete, the computer whiz. Sara had told him about Pete, but had neglected to mention she was a she. He knew that the other men were also assuming she was a Peter and wondered what their reaction would be when they found out. Oh, he thought with a mental rubbing of his hands and a smile, this is going to be so much fun.

CHAPTER FOUR

Dominic was still staying at his old master's home. He was not happy about it, but a promise was a promise. He had promised Colin that he would stick around and help him for as long as Colin needed him to. The work Colin had Dominic doing was much easier now that the realm was beginning to trust the new couple that had taken over.

Colin had fought and beaten the previous master several months ago. He had been there and still couldn't believe the way Colin had simply cut the man down the way he had. It was both awe-inspiring and frightening at the same time.

At first Dominic had thought poor Shade, Colin's mate, was going to go out and drag the reluctant vampires of the realm into Colin's office. Colin had inherited them from the old master and it had taken this long to make the vamps believe he was not going to punish them for every little thing.

The first week had been the hardest on everyone, especially Shade. She was still a day walker, a vampire that could walk in the sunlight without any consequences, just like Sara, Aaron's mate. Shade had made plans to have an antique dealer come in the large mansion to get an estimate on the God-awful furniture that was crowding the house.

The man had taken his time, estimating what was the least amount he could pay her for each piece, unknowingly telling Shade what he could sell it for on the open market because she could read his mind. He had also assumed, like everyone else did, that Shade was alone most of the time in the house. But Colin, since bonding to Shade, had been able to stay up well past noon now, her magic flowing through his veins as well his through hers.

When the dealer had made a pass at the young woman, Colin had nearly torn the man's throat out before Shade could get him to just toss his "cheating, lying ass" out the door, which he took to mean literally and did just that, tossing him head over ass onto the gravel drive. People, especially vampires, tended to sit up and take serious notice of the way a man protected his mate, and that had been the turning point for the others as well.

Now they had a full staff of workers, tearing out the old wall paper, cleaning the house top to bottom. Also, plumbers and carpenters were there as well. In the few months since Colin had challenged and won against the old master, he and Shade had made many improvements. And more and more of the vampires were coming in to meet them rather than Shade dragging them in.

There were also the added workers working on the secondary home that was being built on the back half of the property. It was a very large structure that would have twenty-four bedrooms and twelve full baths on the second and third floors; the main floor would house a nursery, kitchen and dining hall. Around this building were going to be four small duplexes that would each have two or four bedrooms along with a kitchen, bath, and living room.

The building was going to be a complex for battered and abused children. It was going to be called Becca's Place for

Brent's little sister who had been sexually abused and then killed by a werewolf. Becca had only been four years old.

Brent was their adopted son. His mother, Brenda Shell, a drug addict, had been selling her children for sexual favors to keep herself in heroin and anything else she could get her hands on. One night, it had gotten out of control and Becca had been killed and Brent nearly so. Had Colin not stepped in and given him some of his blood, then he too would have died at the hands of the wolf responsible. A few weeks later, during the shooting and kidnapping of Shade, Brenda and Lynn, the alpha bitch of the wolf pack had been killed.

Bradley Wolff, the alpha to the now largest pack in the United States, had insisted on helping both financially and with the construction aspect of the complex. His help had also cleared the way for the many permits and all the red tape they had been asked to file time and again. Sometimes, his help came in the form of expediting through the red tape in city hall. Some of the officials in office were also were and very much in favor of this type of house, as it would be for both paranormal and human children alike. Shade and Sara, along with the help of April Carlovetti, had been interviewing prospective day help for weeks now and were happy with the positive responses they were getting from around the community.

"I think we should get Pete to come out and look at the computer systems wiring we're having installed before they put the walls up. Can you image the mess it will be if we have to tear out walls once we have kids in the house and anything needs to be fixed?" Shade had been talking about this Pete person for days now. Neither Colin nor Dominic had had the occasion to meet him yet and frankly, Dominic was tired of hearing his name.

"Okay. Why don't you have him come out tonight? That way I can finally meet him and tell him what an ass I think he is for taking up all of my mate's time the other day."

Colin had been bitching for days about the amount of time this Pete was taking of Shade's. That was another thing to dislike this guy about, Dominic thought. Pissing off a master was just not done. Dominic decided that as soon as he met him, he was going to deck the nerd.

"Can't, not tonight. Pete and Eon have been over at Sara and Aaron's all day getting their system set up, and I think it was mentioned that there were other jobs to be done as well," Shade said. "And I think they're finishing up there tomorrow, so maybe tomorrow night. I'll ask."

Shade told him this with a strange smile on her face. Dominic was still trying to work out why the goofy face when the Pete fellow was mentioned.

Dominic was supposed to be starting at the other mansion, Aaron's tomorrow night. He would miss this Pete, not that he really cared one way or another. Besides, being around the newly mated couple was driving him nuts. They were always touching each other, kissing it up, and Shade always had this "I've just been fucked" look about her while Colin looked fucked. He wanted to go to Aaron's. At least with Sara being nearly nine months pregnant, they weren't doing it like rabbits anymore. And they had Internet and their Wii was hooked up while Shade was waiting on the almighty Pete to hook it up here. Yeah, he thought, this was perfect timing.

~~~

"See how this is coming into the house? It's going to cause you big problems if someone were to get onto the property and cut your house lines. This is what I would do to make it a lot safer. That pole over there is wood, see? If you were to cut into it behind the transformer and run a secondary line from it, through the pole base then underground and into the house, no one would know to sever it if they tried to cut your power off. The same with the wires running to the house. Leave them there, but have the main source hooked up inside coming in through underground wire housing. You could have the main power switch right in the closed area that you're currently running the security system in. You'd also continue to have a feed from the cameras at all times. No surprises that way, at least to those in the house."

"How would you get the wire harness through the pole? Cutting a hole isn't going to help much with the wires coming out the other side where someone could see them anyway, couldn't they?" Daniel was walking around the property with a recorder and a notebook, and he was sure he was going to miss something Pete said to him.

"These poles are wood and woodpeckers cut into them all the time. You'd just cut holes at different lengths and depths to fish the wiring down that resemble bird holes. It might look wrong up close, but that high up, no one is going to notice. Underground isn't so hard either. You do a pull plug every few feet and fish it the same way. You won't have a trench mark, and the grass is mostly undisturbed as well. You would have to use more wire. Not moving in a direct line of sight to the house would be your best bet, harder to trace that way too if it's all zig-zaggy."

Daniel watched her as she showed him what she meant with each step in the process. He liked that she was easy going and didn't talk down to people.

Daniel had been outside with her for nearly three hours and had learned more in that time about security measures than he could have imaged possible. She was savvy and clever; her thinking was like that of a crook. Daniel liked her ideas and was certain that Aaron would as well. Pete's idea about wiring the electric gate and fences around the property were dead on too. She suggested that they wire the sections in different intervals on different grids of a panel, overlapping the power going to each section. That way a person could not cut one section without a couple more still being hotwired to the same section so that it was still hot in the event of power being cut any one section. And all the while she was talking to him, she was working on the computer wire harness for the indoor house system that would run in through the whole house and not be out in an open area to mess up the deco of the house. Amazing, he thought.

And so was Aaron MacManus. Daniel had finally gotten the nerve to approach the big vamp this morning. He had worried about how he would react to him interfering. He'd never given any reason for Daniel to be afraid of him, but he just didn't want to take any chances. At least until Eon had come along.

"Mr. MacManus, I was wondering if I might have a word with you. It's about the young man, Eon, sir." He stuttered a little, but had been proud of the fact that he hadn't thrown up — yet.

"Daniel, please call me Aaron. And what about him? Oh God, please tell me he hasn't given Brent another sound piece of advice concerning women?"

Daniel laughed and relaxed, which he was sure was what Aaron had meant for him to do. Eon had been a bit...over helpful in his talks with Brent. But a quick word from Pete and he had stopped.

"No. At least not that I'm aware of. Pete talked to Eon about it, but you might want to sensor Duncan for a while.

No, it's about what he is. Eon's a pup, a late bloomer, we call them."

"Eon? Really? I hadn't gotten that from him, but then I've not spent a great deal of time around him. It's not that I don't believe you, but...well, I'm assuming you're here because you want to introduce him to Bradley." Daniel watched the master lean back in his chair and wondered again how the guy could stand the mess on his desk.

"No, sir, I mean yes, sir. Shit! What I mean is I don't think the pup knows. I was talking to him yesterday and he was adopted – a foundling."

Daniel felt like he was screwing this up for the kid. He did not want Aaron to think the kid was stupid; Eon was just ignorant of what he was. Daniel didn't want everyone to find out the hard way when Eon shifted the first time.

"Okay, I'm sorry, but you'll have to explain a few things to me before I understand, all right? First, isn't he a little old to have not realized he's a wolf? Shouldn't he have, well, changed once or twice by now? I would think that'd be a good indicator that he was one." Daniel could see that Aaron was trying to understand and not make fun of his race.

"Yeah, that's what makes him a late bloomer. He would have had training, counseling from his parents or in his case, a mentor. And because he's an adult, when he changes – if he does, then it could possibly kill him. His body hasn't had the conditioning or training it needs to change. Most of us full bloods begin slowly at around puberty; fur first, then maybe our paws or legs. Never a whole change, not until we are ready physically and mentally. We grow up knowing what we are, what were capable of. Eon doesn't have a clue."

"So, then you think that he's not a full blood, that somehow he's been overlooked? Okay. He's not quiet eighteen, and he's never changed. He may or may not change too, right? Tell me what you need for me to do. I'm sorry, I don't know more about your kind, but I'm willing to learn and help him. You, as well. But I would like to caution you about one thing... Pete, she seems very protective of him and I don't want her hurt either. Or for her to hurt you." Aaron grinned and the hair on the back of Daniel's neck stood up. It said, "I think you could hurt her, but you had better fucking not."

"No! I wouldn't hurt either of them. Besides, just between the two of us, I'm a little afraid of her. No, I think she'd hurt me if I even looked at Eon wrong. I was going to ask if I could go to my alpha first. He's the one who'd have the most information for us. And he'd have to accept Eon into the pack if he wanted to stay here."

Daniel worked for Aaron now and felt it would have been an act of betrayal somehow to go back to his alpha about someone within Aaron's domain. Plus, he respected Aaron. Aaron scared him, but he did respect him.

"The fact that you are asking me permission shows me what a great friend you are going to be to Eon. I am honored that you did this for me and for the pup. And I agree you should go to Bradley and tell him. But I'd like to be kept in the loop. And to also be there when you tell Pete. And you are going to tell her, not me. I'm not that stupid."

Somehow, he thought telling Pete was going to be much more difficult than telling Eon he might get furry once a month. But he agreed. Daniel thought he might start making notes to follow when he spoke to the girl. She was all right, but like Aaron said, she was protective. Somewhat like a she-bitch with her cubs.

~~~

Because of the time she had spent outside with Daniel, Pete was late getting out of the house. According to Dunc, she was scheduled to do the other two homes as well when she could work them in, Shade's and then April's. By the time Dominic showed up, Pete was still working in the kitchen pantry with Brent at her heels "helping" her.

"Want me to hold that thingy for ya? I can reach it if I stand on the stool again. I won't almost fall on you this time," Brent asked. Dominic laughed, thinking almost falling on someone was sort of like being almost pregnant.

"Sure, but you need to stand really still this time. I know it's hard, but you almost wobbled us both to the floor that last time."

Dominic stood right outside the little room and listened to the little boy and his new friend. Brent was a great kid and Dominic had already fallen in love with him. The girl, however...he was not aware that Sara had had her friends over to the mansion yet.

"Okay, Pete, I gots it. I mean, I have it. Whew, that's a hard one to remember, isn't it?"

Pete? They had a guy in there too? Shit, the room was not near big enough for one adult and a kid, much less all three of them. As Dominic started forward to see how they had managed it, "Pete" spoke again.

"Yeah, I know, buddy, but you and I will work on it until I leave tonight. You're doing really well. What's the other rule you need to practice?" he heard her ask as they both exited the little pantry.

"I have to say the 'g' when it's on the end of a word. Dominic, look what's...what we have been doing." This time he emphasized the 'g' a little too hard, but he at least remembered.

Dominic just stared at her. Pete. This was Pete. He was not a "he" at all. He was a she, a very beautiful she. He stared at her for too long, Dominic realized, when she looked nervously at Brent. It was then that he noticed she was wearing sunglasses. He realized that he had stopped breathing and as he inhaled deeply, bringing her scent into his lungs, he staggered slightly. Sweet and spicy — cinnamon and nutmeg, he thought.

Dominic looked at her sharply. No, no fucking way. It was the pantry, not her. Yeah, that was it. She was not his mate. Not her, not now, not fucking likely.

Duncan chose that moment to enter the kitchen where the other three had been standing. Duncan bumped into Dominic lightly and it broke the spell that had seemingly come over him.

"Oh, Master Dominic, I did not expect you until tomorrow evening. Master Aaron and Sara have gone into town for some games to play on the weasel...err the gaming toy in the living room. They should be back shortly."

Dominic glanced back at the now closed pantry door where the girl had presumably gone back into, and then at the back door to the outside. Escape, no not escape. Escape was for someone who was trapped and he was not going to be trapped. She was not going to sink her fucking claws into him, thank you very much. Dominic looked at Duncan and realized he had missed whatever he had been saying to him.

"Is there something wrong, sire?"

"She's...I thought...is she Peter the cable guy...err girl? Her, that girl, is she Peter?" he asked, and immediately felt stupid.

"Actually, it's just Pete. And yes, sire, she is most definitely a she." He looked at Duncan's smile and cringed inside.

"How...how long?"

"How long? Well, I believe she's been a girl her whole life, sire." Duncan was not trying to be a smartass. He just answered Dominic's question. But right now it wasn't being helpful. It was being…shit. Pete was his mate.

Dominic took a deep breath, trying to calm himself. It was her. It was her. It was her was all he could think about right now, like a horrific loop going round and round in his head. He felt as if someone had pole axed him. All these centuries, and he comes back to the main house one night early and there she was. He should have stayed away. Now…he would not need to stay away to avoid her. She would just be there, always in the back of his mind. He was not going to have it happen. Not to him, not now, not fucking ever.

Dominic had seen what Colin had gone through and, yeah, it had ended okay for him. But no fucking way was he going to be trapped by a fucking girl, a fucking human girl. Not the same one every fucking night. Fuck!

When Pete came out of the pantry again, he was still standing there, not having any idea why. He was angry. More than angry, he was livid, and she looked pissed, although he could not figure why she would be mad. He was the one who had to have her. She could go her whole life without one thing from him, but he would die without her. Of course he would have to drink from her, feed from her to bond with her, but that was beside the point, he thought angrily. She simply was not allowed to be pissy, damn it. He had been mad first.

"You stay the fuck away from me, do you hear?" He heard himself snarl at her. "I don't want you sniffing around looking for a piece of ass and you sure as shit are not going to be spending eternity with me."

Dominic felt a bit of something touch his skin, hot and painful. He didn't know what it was and he knew in that moment he should have stopped to breathe before he'd spoken to her. He could see her building up, her anger washing over her body like a silken sheet. Her hair sparked and there was a slight light coming from behind the sunglasses she had on. When she stepped toward him and poked her finger into his chest, he almost looked down to see if she had a blade. It hurt that much.

"Why you worthless worm. You...you son of a bitch. What gives you the... I don't care. No one has the right to speak to anyone they've just... I don't know what the fuck you're talking about, but I wouldn't spend five minutes, no, I wouldn't spend five seconds with you if my very fucking life depended on it." She grabbed her coat, flew out the door, and disappeared in the darkness. He made to go after her when suddenly, Brent was standing in front of him.

"Move, kid, I'm not finished with her yet."

Dominic had not meant to snap at Brent, but just then he heard a loud rumble of a motor start up. He wasn't near finished with her yet and she was getting away.

"You were mean, Dominic, and you made her mad. You were mean and there weren't no reason for it. She's my friend and you yelled at her." He watched, stunned, as Brent slammed his small fist into his belly then turned and fled the room, Duncan fast on his heels.

Well, just great, he thought. He had handled that very nicely. Stupid, stupid, stupid! Cursing himself, Dominic left the house. He suddenly felt as though he did not deserve to be around anyone right now. And what the fuck was Sara going to say?

CHAPTER FIVE

Pete called the house the next afternoon, hoping that the master of the house was gone and Duncan would answer. He did and she was so relieved that she couldn't speak for several seconds.

"Hello, is anyone there?" Duncan asked.

"Hi Dunc, it's Pete. I was wondering if I could please come by and get my tools and my bag? I left in kind of a hurry last night and walked off and forgot to get them."

Pete was so hoping he wouldn't mention why she had left in a hurry, or worse, ask her what she had said to his master to piss him off like that. She thought him the rudest of all men. If he was Mrs. Sara's husband or mate whatever Brent had called him, then Pete could only feel sorry for her and their kids.

"Oh, Miss Pete, I'm so sorry about last night. I do not know what to say about Master Dominic. He has never —"

She cut him off before he could say much more. "Duncan, I so really don't want to talk about it, if that's okay with you. Do you think I could come by and get my things? I don't want to get you into trouble or anything, but I need my tools. They're kind of expensive and I'd be hard pressed to replace all of them. Plus, there's a lot of them I've had made or made myself. I can be there in an hour. I'm at one of my part-timers now, but I'll be done in a few."

"Yes, miss, please come and get them. Master Dominic is...he is not able to be up and about right now, so you coming in an hour will suit just fine. I will be expecting you, as will the missus. She would like to have a word with you, if you would not mind. She feels very badly about what transpired last evening."

Pete did not want to talk to the missus or anyone else in that bedlam. The more she had thought about it, the more she thought the missus' husband or mate or whatever the hell he was, was nuts.

"Is she going to hold my stuff hostage if I don't want to talk to her? Because I gotta tell you, Dunc, the thought of talking to her or that fucking mate of hers, that makes my belly turn up. I don't want to speak to anyone. I know they hired me for a job, and I'll finish it for them, but only if and when that 'master' isn't up. I just want my shit, but if I have to leave it or talk with her, then I'd just as soon replace it. So you tell Missus that I said thanks but no thanks. See ya." And she hung up.

Pete sat on her bed ten minutes later and thought about the people there. Sara seemed all right, a little bossy and a bit nosey, but it wasn't anything Pete couldn't ignore if she wanted. Duncan was fun and she found herself cleaning up her language when she was around him. Brent was a great kind and she was already half in love with him. That Aaron guy was okay. She didn't know what he was to the household, but thought he was someone important to them. But the guy from last night, Pete thought him the rudest of them all. She wondered what their kids would have to grow up with as him as a dad.

~~~

Aaron was in the half room, the room between the dining room and the living room, with Sara enjoying the quiet of the house with her before he had to retire for the day. That's where Penny, the cook, found him. He looked up at her when she entered.

Since bonding and mating with Sara, his ability to withstand more of the sun had increased. Everyone, himself included, thought that it was because of her magical blood running through his veins. He did not really care; he just loved being with her more.

"Your ladyship, lordship, there's something wrong with Mr. Duncan. I found him in my kitchen just sitting there holding the phone. He's all pale, even for him, and I don't think he's breathing at all. I took one look at him and thought you should come see him. I think he's dead, poor old thing."

"No, we couldn't be so lucky, Penny. He's only playing opossum. But let's go see what the fuss is about. It's probably because we left the kitchen in a mess again last night, my dear. You wait and see if it isn't."

Aaron loved watching Sara eat human food, and she had had a craving for another cheeseburger and fries last night. Watching her eat had always been a major turn on for him; her as well for that matter. He got another erection just thinking about the fun they'd had in the kitchen. He grinned, thinking that it would be worth whatever Duncan wanted to appease him this time.

Aaron reached out to Duncan as he walked toward the kitchen. The sorrow and hurt Duncan was feeling hit him with such force that Aaron flashed to the kitchen just ahead of Sara. Duncan was still sitting in the chair where Penny had said he was, still holding the phone tucked against his ear, staring out into the room, a blank look on his face.

51

"Duncan? What is it, old man?" Aaron knelt in front of him and gently took the phone from his grip and handed it backwards to Sara who was standing just behind him.

"She will not come...he...they were so mad. I tried to get her to come and get her 'shit.' She called it her shit, sire. I do not think I will understand that one. And, oh Missus, I told her that you wanted to speak to her, that you would let her have her things if she would speak to you. I never meant for it to sound like a... It was not a threat. No, I only wanted her to come here. I thought... I do not know what happened between them, Miss Pete and Master Dominic; they were so very angry. I thought maybe you could find out...and poor little Brent, he was crying, sobbing really. She did not slow down to tell him good-bye, you see. Master Dominic had made Miss Pete so upset. She did not say good-bye to Brent. Now...now, she will not come here. Oh, sire, I believe I have let the pooch screw us."

"Duncan, who was mad at Pete? Was it Brent? Did she make him mad?"

Aaron had really liked Pete, but if she did anything to Brent, the girl would not be able to hide far enough nor deep enough, because he would find her and make her pay. That little guy was the world to all of them in his Kiss. He would also deal with the pooch incident and whatever Duncan had meant by that later. Right now, he needed to get to the bottom of this.

"No, sire, not Brent. Master Dominic and Miss Pete, they had the fight. She was in the pantry working, you see. She and Brent were installing the wire saddle for the weasel. He...well, he just attacked her verbally as soon as she came into the room. He said that he did not want to see her, for her not to expect anything about his ass, and something about an eternity. I believe I might have missed some of that, now that

I think about it. I thought they knew each other, that he felt she was stalking him for some reason. But he had asked me if she was a girl, like he had not realized that until that moment, so that could not be it, could it? Master Dominic would have known if she was a female if she was stalking him, would he not, sire?"

"Yes, I believe you're right. He would have had to have noticed Pete being a girl. Dominic was here while Pete was? I thought he wasn't due back until tomorrow." Aaron looked at Penny then Sara, and neither seemed to know either. "Duncan, tell me exactly what you remember. It's important for me to understand." Aaron thought he had a pretty good idea, but wanted to be sure before he got too excited.

"He told her not to sniff at his ass and that he was not going to be spending eternity with her. She seemed to think spending only five seconds in his acquaintanceship was too much. I cannot say that I blame her on that. He was a bit harsh with her, if you do not mind my saying so. The poor miss, he seemed...well, unhinged, even to me. Oh, sire, the hatred that came from them. Miss Pete left right away, the poor little mite. And Brent, he was so angry with Dominic, he screamed at him, telling him to go get her. Master Dominic left right as her motor bike started. I thought it was to get Miss Pete to come back for Brent, but that didn't happen. Then this morning when she called, she said that she did not need her things bad enough to have to talk about what had happened. She would not talk to either of you." Duncan started to stand then dropped back into the chair. "Oh, my lord! I believe that she thinks you are him, that Dominic is the master of the house not you. She said you were nuts. She thinks...oh master, what have I done?" Duncan look so devastated that Aaron pulled him into a hug to comfort him.

"You did nothing wrong, Duncan, nothing at all. But I think I understand better what happened between them. I think that Pete, much to the horror of our Dominic, is his mate. We've all heard what he thinks about having one. The sameness of it, night after night, the same woman for all of eternity, he believes it to be a fate worse than the sun. Her special scent for him must have hit him when she came out of the pantry, or it was already throughout the house when he got here. And I can see him taking it out on her. It's hard on a vampire after all these years, sometimes centuries, of being alone to finally find the one who would complete you. When he thought Pete to be a boy, it must have thrown him."

"Mate or not, he had no right to attack her, Aaron. We have to make him apologize to her, or at the very least get her things back to her. We can't make him claim her, but he damn well isn't going to hurt her in the process." Sara's voice was hard and unforgiving. Her fierce protectiveness for the little human did not surprise Aaron. That was one of the many, many things he loved about her.

Aaron knew from his own experience with finding Sara and denying the attraction what would happen to Dominic if he did not claim Pete as his mate now that he had found her. He would slowly go insane until he became rogue, someone without remorse, killing humans and other vampires alike just for the fun of it. It would be a long and very slow process. Dominic would, in the beginning, make Pete crazy by stalking her and driving others away he felt were trying to move in on her even as he protested wanting or needing her. Then Dominic's protective instinct would go into overdrive and Aaron was not sure how Pete would react to that. Knowing the girl, Aaron had a feeling it would not be easy on either of them, but Dominic needed to be dealt with and face the consequences.

54

"I'll deal with Dominic as soon as I find him. Sara, love, we need to let Pete know that she can come here without harm and that Dominic is not demented or the master of this realm. And that we would like her to come and get her things, plus finish the jobs she started for us. Duncan, find out how Brent is, please, and make sure he understands that we are going to make sure that things are fixed and that his friends will be all right as well. All right, we all have our assignments, but I must retire."

Duncan cleared his throat before addressing Aaron. "Miss Pete has never had a home cooked meal before, sire. I don't have any clue what that would even be in terms of human food, but do you think it would be all right if Miss Penny fixed Miss Pete one?"

Penny had been told a few weeks after she had moved into the little cottage by the mansion that she worked for vampires and other magical creatures. They did not want her to become suspicious of certain things that may go on within the walls of Aaron's Kiss. Penny just put her fist on her ample hip and said that she was not born yesterday and she was pretty sure this family was not the first bunch of bloodsuckers she had worked for, but at least this one was honest and up front about what they were. Aaron had laughed for days.

"Yes, Duncan, that's an excellent idea. You go ahead. Between the two of you, I'm sure she'll be very happy with the results."

Aaron was still grinning as he made his way to his lair in the sublevels of their home. Poor Dominic, Aaron thought, he was certainly in for it now.

CHAPTER SIX

"I'm here to see Pete, is she here?" Toby was her last resort.

Sara had been everywhere looking for Pete and leaving messages for her to call at every place she went. The people at the house said they had not seen her today. Booger had said that she was there last evening and then again that morning, but he had not seen her since. But, he said, she was pretty mad when he had seen her last, and no, he did not know what was up.

"She's out on one of her part-timers, Mrs. MacManus. But if you'd like for me to, I can see if I can get her a message," Toby said.

Sara reached out to Toby, touching him mentally, and found that Pete had not said anything to this man about what had happened at the house when she had spoken to him last night. But he did know where Pete was most of the other times.

Duncan would not give Sara the phone number to Pete's drop n' kick phone when she has asked. He said that Pete had trusted him with it and he was not breaking that trust. Sara didn't push. Duncan was upset enough. He had tried to call it and left a message for Pete to call Sara twice already.

Sara was afraid that Pete was out of minutes with her phone service and couldn't retrieve the messages anyway. Sara was about to give up until Dominic could be found, which was proving to be as difficult as finding Pete. Aaron had checked his lair that Dominic was using while staying with them, but Dominic had not been there at all last night, or today.

"Toby, I really need to speak with Pete. It's very important that I reach her as soon as possible. Here is my cell number and my house number as well. I have her things and her money. Could you make sure she gets both, please?"

Toby looked at the envelope she was holding out to him and then looked at her with a frown. She didn't need anyone else upset with her right now. She was too emotional as it was and she wasn't feeling well today.

"Ma'am, you don't know Pete well if you think she'll be expecting a payment from you. I don't know what happened, but you coming in here like this and having her tools tells me it wasn't good." He stared at her for a few seconds then turned away. "Come with me, and let me show you something."

Sara followed him to the back of the store where there were two desks in a medium-sized office. One was a complete mess of papers stacked haphazardly on books and catalogs, old coffee mugs full of pins and such. There were also pens and sandwich wrappers mingled in with invoices and bills. It looked a great deal like Aaron's desk at home, she thought.

The other desk was a major contrast. The bulletin board had a calendar and a few business cards stuck to it in neat order with all the same colored push pins. The desk was devoid of anything other than a phone, a clean doodle pad, and a container of pencils all sharpened to the same height. There was a pretty and healthy African violet in the deepest shade of blue Sara had ever seen sitting on the far corner, as far away from the messy one as it could get. The desk was polished to a bright sheen and the chair was pushed in straight against the desk.

"Which one do you think is mine?" he asked her with a grin. "I can tell she was here last night or this morning because the plant is watered. There is never anything out of place even when she's sitting here, or left out when she leaves. Now, you're thinking to yourself, 'why should I care what her desk looks like?' Look at her calendar. See what she has written on it. You'll understand a little more."

Toby left her to look all she wanted. Sara wandered over to the little desk and sat in the chair. She took the calendar off the wall, pulled it toward her, and began flipping through the dates to read the notes written on there.

January 10th-paid for SC doctor bill//BAL $6000

January 16th –paid $100 to ML//BAL $2500

February 2nd –paid $600 to ML//BAL $9000

March 10th –Rec'd $10//BAL $604

May 16th –Birthday $18//BAL $22

The only time there seemed to be an increase in the balance column was when the balance dropped below one hundred dollars. A couple of days before each major balance decrease, there was an appointment for work, a company, and time. It appeared Pete would work for a larger company only when necessary to the balance of her income. Then nearly every penny was spent before she would start all over. Sara leaned over and opened the top drawer. There was nothing in it but a box of unopened pencils—who used pencils anymore?—a huge bag of paper clips and one of rubber bands. The second drawer held a file box, which Sara took out and set on the desk.

Opening it, she found what the initials meant. Pete was paying bills for others, not her own. All the money Pete earned other than what she absolutely needed to live on went to someone else in need. Electric bills that were near shut off were paid, phone bills in danger of having service cut off, paid. There were hundreds of them, hospital, dentist, bookstore bill at the local college, birthday money for at least twenty kids, their names and dates in monthly order with their addresses with them. And toward the end of the list was Becca's Home. Pete was putting money when she could into the account Bradley had set up for the pack businesses to donate to. And it looked as though she had been doing it for some time.

To date, Pete had given over eight thousand dollars to the account in addition to the other monies she was giving out. Sara sat there stunned, hardly able to believe what she was seeing. The dates for the contributions to Becca's Home and the date that she had been called by Duncan were months apart. Pete had known who all of them were long before coming out to the house or meeting them in the parking lot that first day. Sara got up to find Toby.

"Why did you show these to me? I'm impressed, beyond impressed, but I don't understand why you'd show me something that seems so private to her."

"I wanted you to know she's trustworthy. You and your friends the other day, that's the most I have ever seen her talk to anyone, and I don't know that I'd ever heard her laugh before. Then you come in today upset and demanding, and yeah, you demanded to see her. She is more special than any woman I've ever met and the most unsung hero as well. Those papers you found in there? They aren't even a drop in the bucket of what she does around the area. When I told you she helps out, I wasn't kidding you. She does so much for all of us. I just wanted you to know her. I'll take her tools now, but I won't take the money. If you want the money to go somewhere, there's this new home she was telling me about. It's called...let me see, ah yeah, Becca's Place. You send them the money. She'd like that."

Tears blurred in her eyes, Sara had never been as touched by anything as she was by the fact that these people knew about Becca's Place and were so willing to give to it. And to give to it in the name of someone else.

"Yes, yes, I'll send the money to the house. They can really use all they can get, I'm sure." Sara left knowing that if Dominic did not make this right, she might have to stake him herself.

CHAPTER SEVEN

Sara, Shade and Mel met for lunch at the local Mexican restaurant at noon that same day. Sara had just finished telling them about the whole incident with Pete and Dominic and ended with her handing the money over to Shade she had intended to give to Pete for the work she had already completed.

Shade was grateful for the money. She still had problems just spending money even though Colin had assured her that he could build her twenty houses like the one they were building for Becca, but old habits die hard, Sara knew that first hand.

"Where is this girl now, do you know? And Dominic? Has Aaron had any luck with finding him either? You know Brent was really quiet when he came home that day. He went straight to bed without saying a word about what happened. But the next morning, he seemed fine when I dropped him off at school. I wonder why Dominic would have such an issue with Pete being his mate. She's very beautiful, smart, generous, and willing to take him on. That right there says a lot about her fortitude. I wish that I could have seen her getting all up and personal with him," Shade said with a grin.

Sara had wished the same thing. Duncan said that Pete did not back down at all, but had poked her finger right in Dominic's chest as though she meant business. Sara loved that Pete could and would stand up to the jerk. She loved Dominic, but right now, she wasn't very happy with him.

Pete was beautiful, Sara thought again. Her hair was dark brown with a short and sassy cut that spiked out all over her head. She was really tall and most of that was leg, Sara discovered when Pete had climbed the ladder yesterday. Her skin was creamy and smooth, her nose was a small button, and her cheeks were high and rosy. Her perfectly arched eyebrows were a little darker than her hair. Her eyes, when a person was privileged to see them, were polished silver. The color was a gorgeous contrast to her dark hair and light skin color. Aaron had told Sara that he had never seen anyone with eyes that color before, and that was saying a lot. Sara wondered what people had said to make Pete feel the need to wear sunglasses all the time.

Sara shifted on her seat again. She was miserable and tired. And she felt...not sick, but just something. She was startled when Mel asked her about it.

"What's with you? Something is wrong, what?"

She was surprised. Sara could usually keep such a tight hold on her mind and emotions, but was having a hard time concentrating on it today for some reason.

"I'm just tired, nothing much," Sara said. And she was too. All this moving about was exhausting her, and she decided that was it. She was doing more today. All she wanted to do was to eat and go home and take a long nap.

Suddenly, there was a disturbance at the door of the restaurant and Pete was standing there, searching the room. When her eyes landed on Sara, she started toward her. A chill ran down Sara's back. Something was wrong, very wrong.

"We need to go, you and me. We need to go. Right now, Mrs. MacManus, we have to go," Pete said in way of a greeting, completely ignoring the other women.

Sara felt something twist inside of her. The babies, something was wrong with the babies.

"Oh God, something is wrong, isn't it?"

She watched as Pete turned to the waitress that had just taken their order and said, "Há um lugar que eu posso tomar meu amigo? Seu bebê vem agora mesmo." Pete turned back to Sara and looked worried, even to Sara. "Anna is going to help me take you to a back room. The babies are in trouble and you need to move right now."

~~~

"I didn't know you could speak Spanish. What did you tell her?" Sara was starting to babble. Pete practically had to drag her along with her. Pete let her talk. It mattered little what she was saying as long as Sara kept moving with her.

"It wasn't Spanish, it's Portuguese. You're not in a Mexican restaurant. You know that, don't you?" Sara was moving, but not fast enough. "I asked her if there was somewhere we could go. You're in labor." Pete turned again to the girl hovering over her.

"Fala inglês?" She answered that she did not speak English, but there was a lady in the kitchen who spoke both very well. Pete asked her to go and bring her to them please.

"No, this is Mexican. I eat here all the time. I love their number two. It's 'Costeletas de cordeiro enchidas grelhadas com arroz marrom.' Then we have Pão doce for dessert. I know what I eat." Pete noticed that Sara had to stop to breathe through the pain every couple of steps now.

"You're eating grilled stuffed lamb chops with brown rice, and your dessert is called sweet bread. It's Portuguese, trust me. We have to talk...well, I have to talk, and you have to shut up and not say a word." Pete laid Sara down on the floor as she spoke to her.

"You know you could be just a tad nicer in your requests, I think. We're all nervous and you making demands is frankly scaring the crap out of me. You just need to tone it down a couple of notches, please," Mel said to Pete.

Pete looked at Sara and winked. Pete didn't care what Mel thought about her as long as she helped when she needed her to and moved when she was in her way.

"How do we even know what you're saying is true? And another thing, how did you just happen by? Were you at one of your 'part-timers' again? Why is it that you can't get a full time job? Is it because of your attitude? No, say it isn't so! Not you, you are so sweet and friendly —"

"Oh yeah, you have such a hard job, don't you, queenie? For your information, no one can afford to have me on staff full time. I'm too good at what I do. What the fuck do you do? Wave your fingers and stuff just happens? Yeah, I can see where that would just tire you out."

"For your information, I am a queen, you insolent bitch. I'm the queen of all the magic in the universe in several worlds. What could you possibly do that would require so much money that you can't be employed? Hooking?" Just as Pete started to stand up and knock Mel on her queenie ass, Sara screamed.

"Enough! Shade, come over here and help me. Mel, either go to Aaron or home. I'm in pain, lots of pain, and you two bickering is not helping me. You." Sara pointed at Pete. "You tell me what you want me to do, and drop the attitude. I'm in no mood for you either."

Sara was stressing out and Pete could not let her do that. Things were going to be bad enough. But if Sara started freaking out, it could be the death of all three of them. Pete took in a deep breath and slowly let it out with all her anger.

"Devo você trazer me algumas toalhas ou cobertores, agora. Por favor?" While the young woman brought the towels that Pete had asked for, she turned back to Sara and Shade.

"You have to listen to me very carefully and not to say a single word. The life of your son depends on it."

Sara whimpered but did not speak. She did reach out and take Shade's hand and put it over her mouth, as if to say "help me" then Sara nodded to Pete.

"How this works is that we have to make an exchange of trust. You must trust me to save your children and I will trust you with my secret of what I can do." When Sara started to speak, Pete stopped her. "No, now listen. The cord is wrapped tightly around your son's throat. If it isn't removed now, he will strangle and die. The little girl will die as well because he cannot move on his own and she can't be born soon enough to allow her to live."

"She's a true immortal, she can't die," Shade blurted.

"She will if she doesn't take her first breath." Pete looked at Shade then at Sara. "I can save them both, but we need to trust, fully trust each other, Mrs. MacManus. If you don't fully trust that I will save them then do not say yes. That's really important that you believe in me. In exchange, I will trust you with me. When I open the door and let myself go, I will reach into you and unwind the cord from his neck. Then I will have to deliver them both. There isn't time to get you anywhere else. It's me, only me, understand so far?"

Pete waited, knowing that the women would need to talk amongst themselves first. As they were friends, she expected no less.

"What's she telling you is true. If the babies don't breathe, then they aren't immortal. Immortality doesn't begin if there is no life to begin with," Mel said to Sara as she paced the room. "I still don't like this, any of this. But I would trust her. Not many humans know that information. Not that I think she's fully human anymore, but I would trust her, Sara."

"If I ask you something, is it the same as Sara asking it?" Shade asked Pete.

"You can ask me anything you like. But the ultimate answer, the trust, has to come from Sara as long as you both understand that. And queenie, I don't like this anymore than you do. But I do appreciate the vote of confidence."

"What are you?" Shade asked her quietly.

Pete looked at Shade and then turned away. Pete had a long list of things people had been calling her all her life, but she was sure that was not what Shade was asking her. But she still was not sure how to answer the question because she didn't know either.

"I'm just me. I don't...I don't know, just some sort of freak of nature that has no business... We have to hurry Mrs. MacManus. Will you trust me, as I will trust you?"

Sara reached up and took off Pete's sunglasses, startling all of them. "I need to see you. All of you. Yes, please take my trust, as you have given me yours."

Pete nodded once and with a wink said, "Brace yourself, Effie." And she opened the door to everything she was.

Chapter Eight

Dominic woke up to Aaron banging on his door. He tried ignoring it, but Aaron would not fucking stop. When he finally rolled out of the bed and got the door open, he was pretty pissed off. He had gotten in minutes before sunrise and had planned to go out as soon as he could sneak past the household. He was sure they had heard about what had transpired between him and Pete, and to be honest, he was not really happy with himself about it right now either. What had he been thinking jumping all over her like that? He had convinced himself that he didn't really smell her scent of nutmeg and cinnamon, which now that he thought about it, was an odd scent for a mate to give off, although it suited her just fine.

"About fucking time. I can't get to Sara and she's in labor. If I fucking can't sleep, then you aren't going to either. We have some things to discuss anyway. Meet me in my office in thirty minutes or face my wrath. And right now, I'm hoping you don't show up on your own." Dominic watched as Aaron turned on his heel and left him standing there.

Dominic didn't even try to deny that they needed to talk. He just shut the door, turned around, and got dressed. Might as well face the fact that he had fucked up big time, he thought, and get this over with. Hiding out was certainly not getting him anywhere. Pete was a friend of the family and he had screamed at her like a maniac. And the kid, shit, he had even made little Brent cry. But the little bugger had stood up to him, told him that he should go get her and make it right. Brent had even punched him a couple of times. That made him smile despite being worried about what punishment he would have to endure from his master. Dominic took a deep, calming breath and then left the sublevels to face the music.

"Sire? I know what I did was wrong. I don't know what came over me. Well, I do, and I think I'm probably wrong about that anyway. I just thought that I had her scent, you know... But I was wrong. Women don't smell like that to their mates, that couldn't be right. So I've decided that I jumped to conclusions and she isn't my mate. She can't be my mate and smell like a spice like nutmeg. But now that I think on it, though, it suits her. She's a vicious little thing, and once her temper went off...Christ, she has a hell of a temper. That smell had to come from the pantry. It was all over her. That's why it was so strong; she was working in there, Duncan said. The smell of nutmeg and cinnamon was wafting from there..." Dominic stopped talking. He had run down actually. He looked up sharply when he realized that Aaron was laughing at him. That set his temper soaring again and he glared at the older vampire. That didn't do anything but make Aaron laugh harder.

"So, what is this smell that came from the pantry that was all over her? Nutmeg, you say? Yeah, I can see that. And like you, I could see nutmeg as something I would associate with her since I heard that she took Mel on just today. Pissed the queen right off too. Yeah, I think you're right. She isn't your mate. Tell me something, though, is she pretty? I've always thought she was quite beautiful myself." Dominic didn't like where this was going. "You know Bradley, the wolf alpha, is looking for a few women to turn for his pack. Sounds like she could hold her own as a bitch."

No way, Dominic thought. No way was she going to be turned for someone else. When Aaron pulled out his cell and mumbled about pack phone numbers, Dominic flashed across the room and had Aaron pinned against the wall before he thought of what the consequences would be.

"She'll not be turned for anyone but me," he snarled. "You will not call the alpha, do you hear me?" He heard a low growl and it was seconds before he realized that it came from him.

"So, she's not your mate, huh?"

Dominic realized that his fangs had dropped and he had almost unleashed his beast, his eyes turning to the red haze of anger. He knew because he was seeing things in a red haze. "Fuck you." He dropped Aaron to the floor none too gently and stormed to the kitchen and away from the truth. Aaron's laughter followed him all the way into the darkened room.

The entire house was dark during the daylight hours. Aaron had had window shades put on the outside of the house as soon as he had moved in. The solid steel shades would come down and seal against the house as soon as the sun rose, acting as a block against the dangerous rays and a safety measure for the inhabitants while they slept. If anyone wanted some light, as Sara sometimes did, there was a beautifully maintained solarium on the south side of the house.

~~~

As soon as Pete finished the line Robin Williams said in Mrs. Doubtfire, she dropped her shield. Her magic enveloped Sara in warmth and comfort. Pete took Sara's pain away and held it to her. Doing that, Pete felt Sara relax. As Pete laid her hand over Sara's swollen belly, she felt the power race down her arm and light emanated from the tips of her fingers.

Pete knew she was taking a big chance, opening herself up literally like this, but she also knew there was no way she could let the babies die. It just saddened her that she would need to move again and not see these two grow up. But she could not let the others find her. Not now, not ever.

"I need to move into you now. No, don't tense up. You aren't going to feel a thing, I promise. I've taken all of your pain and worry and have set it aside. I want you to relax or I can't move through you. For now, I need you to focus on my voice, listen to the calm tones I'm using, the way my voice is soft and warm. I can see your children, and if you close your eyes, you'll see everything I see. See the little boy, see the cord there? I'm going to remove it now."

As Pete worked, she explained each step to Sara and through her, Shade. When she felt that she had done all she could, Pete began to pull out of Sara's body and gently touch each child as she left. When Pete opened her eyes, Mel was standing next to Sara with the man. Slightly dizzy with exhaustion, Pete took a few seconds to realize who he was. She had met him in the study the other night.

"Aaron, how, what are you doing here? Mel? How are you here? It's daylight. Please, love, go back to the mansion. It isn't safe for you here," Sara said.

Pete looked at first to Sara then the man. Love? Pete was too tired and too muddled to understand what was going on, but she had a feeling she was seeing the master of the house and the mate to Sara. Pete was confused. If this was her mate then who was the asshole from the house?

"I'm still at home, sweetheart. Mel has brought me here to see our babies being born. She didn't want me to miss this event. Her magic is holding me here. I love you very much."

Pete was still trying to work out the dynamics and almost missed what the man was asking of her. She was so tired she couldn't concentrate on him for several seconds. "I'm sorry, sir. What did you say? I was…I didn't hear you."

"You do look very tired, my dear. I said it will soon be dark enough for us to join you here. I don't suppose you could slow it down just a bit for me, Pete?"

"The children are very anxious to meet you both, but I'll speak with them for you. They want to be born. I could wait until you have someone…a real doctor come for them now if you'd prefer."

"No. No, you need to do this for me, for us. I want you to bring them into the world. I will have Thomas, our physician, come, but you will need to finish. Sara and I both want you to finish this for us."

Sara nodded.

With her shields down, Pete now knew what they were. Vampire. The word vampire had never entered her mind when dealing with these people. The bitchy woman, Queenie, was something completely different and she had the same feelings about the two women too. Somehow, they were the same thing, magic and vampire.

Pete moved her hand over the mound of life and closed her eyes, asking for them to wait for their father.

She turned her attention back to the man and said, "Sire, they will wait for you, but the little girl said not to be too long. Also, she said to tell you that she's given permission to the male to be born first, but she will still be the boss over him no matter how big he gets for his pants."

Aaron, a fourteen hundred year old vampire, master of his own realm, with over one thousand people looking to him for protection and guidance, burst into tears. Life could suddenly get no better than this moment in time, he told her.

"Tell the young lady that I have no doubt that she will be just like her mother in all things. Thank you, Pete. I will forever—"

"I need to go. I need to get something from the kitchen. Excuse me."

Pete did not want to hear whatever he had to say. She wasn't much for praise. It embarrassed her in ways she could not explain. She was more of the behind the scenes kind of person. Do the job and get the heck out of Dodge. She turned back to Sara as she stood up. She had to prepare the woman for the birth and blocked everything else from her thoughts.

"Mrs. MacManus, when the time comes, you won't be able to feel the contractions so you will need to bear down and push when I tell you to. It is important that you start when I tell you and stop when I tell you. I don't want to take chances with you or the boy now. You can trust that I won't harm either of you still. Our bargain is still in place. If you'd like to change your mind, I can maybe hold them off until someone else gets here, but I can't be positive."

Pete watched as Sara patted Shade's arm and then nodded when Shade raised her hand. It was funny really and she grinned at her.

"Sara wants to know if she can talk to you now. She said she doesn't want to break the contact between the two of you, but she'd really like to talk to you."

"Yes, you may answer now. Our contact is closed enough to be considered complete that I doubt it would matter anyway. To be honest, I didn't believe you could do it. It must have been very difficult for you to remain quiet for that long." Pete grinned wider when Sara glared at her.

Sara, nodding, tears glistening in her eyes, said, "There are no words adequate enough to thank you for what you've done for me, for us. I thank you for my children and for your trust. If you ever need anything, ever, you'll have it."

Pete started to say something, but could not. No one had ever said anything like that to her before. Not that she had ever given them the chance. She felt the room closing in on her and moved to the door. She needed to escape. Right now, she needed to get away.

Forty-five minutes later, Aaron and Duncan entered the little room, taking up a large portion of it and the air. Duncan was pressed into helping get the extra people out of the room, leaving the members of the Kiss and Pete. Colin, Shade's mate, would be by shortly with the extra car needed to get them home and was going to meet them there as soon as he could. Brent was with Penny and waiting for the news of the new baby.

Everyone seemed ready for the little ones to be born. Now Pete needed to see if the little ones were ready too.

"All right, Mrs. MacManus, I need you to bear down hard and push from your bottom. Push like you need a good poop. I know that sounds gross, but that's where you need to use all the muscles to work from. Sire, you will kneel here and I will hand you your babies as they come. Ready? Push. Push hard."

Seven hard pushes later, baby boy MacManus was born. He was a little guy and the horrific bruise around his tiny neck brought home how close he had come to death. He screamed his first cry when Pete held him upside down by his feet and slapped him a good one across the bottom. Once he took air into his healthy lungs, he quieted.

"I've asked him not to cry too much for the first few days to give his throat time to heal better. His sister has agreed, quite readily actually, to cry for him when he needs something. She has told me to tell you to check him first when she cries, it's probably for him anyway. She is going to be a handful, I think." Pete looked at the baby and saw that he was going to be fine.

His father held him like a precious jewel. Eighteen minutes later, baby girl MacManus came into the world just like the diva she was probably going to turn out to be. She did not scream, but growled like a pro when Pete paid her bottom the same treatment she gave her brother's.

Duncan, good man that he was, had remembered to bring the bags for the birth that the Missus had had ready for some weeks now, so they were able to bundle the babies in diapers and clothes. They were tiny and other than the bruising, were beautiful.

While the families were surrounding the children cooing and awing over them, Pete looked around the room. The hair on the back of her neck had begun to prickle since she finished with the birth. She looked for the source and spotted the man from the kitchen at the MacManus' home standing in the corner away from her. He was staring at her. Well, glaring would be a better term for what he was doing.

Pete turned away and stood, making ready to leave. She did not need anything from him, especially since she had done nothing wrong in the first place, she thought. And she was damn well not going to listen to him if he decided to go off again.

The doctor would be there soon, and they would be moving everyone to the mansion as soon as he checked them all over. Pete was nearly to the door when Mrs. MacManus stopped her. Pete reached out to grip the shelf nearest to her to steady herself, exhaustion and hunger hitting her hard just at that moment. If she didn't leave soon, she was afraid she wouldn't. At least not until she took a long nap.

"Pete, you'll come back to the house with us. I would like you to stay with us for a few days. You look a little wrung out."

Sara didn't make it sound like a request, but a direct order. Pete was not intimidated. She could say "no" better than she could "yes" when she needed to.

"I don't think so, but thanks. I have a part-timer tomorrow morning, and I need to get home now. You all should be fine and I'm sure the doctor will have whatever you guys need. I have to get going."

Pete looked at Mel, daring her to say something about her job, but Mel only nodded and went back to touching the little girl in her arms. Pete moved closer to the door and was proud of the fact that she had only staggered twice more on her way through to the kitchen.

Pete felt the man move toward her, but decided not to acknowledge him in any way. She knew now he was a part of the family somehow, but he was not Sara's mate. Not that it mattered to her one way or the other. With her walls back up, Pete was not even sure if he was like them or not, and didn't care either way. She didn't think he was any less insane than she had before.

The Hangchows, owners and cooks of the restaurant, stopped her twice on her way out. Once to thank her for the blessing she had placed upon their establishment with the birth of the twins. It seemed that their equivalent of her Mother Nature blessed households where healthy children were born as not many survived were they had lived. The second was to ask if she could take a delivery to Booger for them. She agreed. She was going that way anyway and went ahead and paid for it for him. The man followed her closely as she left by the back door of the restaurant. She turned sharply and glared at him.

"I want you to go away and leave me alone. No matter what you think, I didn't take anything from the MacManus' or Mr. Hangchow. I'm not a thief. The food is for someone who lives at the house I live at and he had placed an order. I'm just delivering it for him. And right now, I don't have the energy to deal with whatever you think you might have to say to me. I want you to stay the fuck away from me. You're insane."

Pete could feel the sting of the tears in her eyes, and decided that she was just overly tired. She knew that he followed her to the door and out to her bike, but she chose to ignore him. It wasn't as if he was speaking to her anyway. She loaded the food bag into the back of the bike's saddle bag, and threw her leg over the seat.

"I'd like to have a word with you, please. I think I might have said some things the other night that may have been a little rude and I—"

"You may have said some things that were rude? Are you fucking nuts? You attacked me, you stupid asshole. I didn't even know you existed and you came at me as if I was...I was some sort of stalker or something. You need to have your head examined. And stay the hell away from me."

Before she could say anything else to him, or start the engine, he touched her forehead with the palm of his hand and simply said, "Sleep."

CHAPTER NINE

When Pete woke up the, she didn't know where she was. She sat up slightly and looked around. The room was nice with lots of old but beautiful furniture. The bed she was in was huge and smelled like warm nights.

Now I am nuts, she thought and started to rise. She saw him then, sitting in a dark wingback chair staring at her intently. She didn't speak to him but got up anyway, as she really needed to use the bathroom.

Throwing off the heavy comforter, she swung her long legs to the floor and stood up. She staggered only a little, caught herself, and took a step toward the bath. He was in front of her in a flash. Pete put her hands out to stop her forward momentum, but still hit him in the chest. She looked up at him and saw that his eyes had started to change to a deep red.

"Are you like them, like the MacManus's?" she asked before she remembered she was not going to speak to him.

"A vampire. Yes, I'm a vampire. Are you afraid of me?"

There was a weird cadence to his voice, she noticed. It was husky and deep. As much as she hated to admit it, she liked the way it made her feel — warm and protected, nothing like he had actually made her feel in real life.

"No. I have to pee, and if you'll move, I'll take care of that right now." She moved to the right at the same time he did to the left. The same move occurred when she moved left. "Do you mind? I want to use the facilities."

He looked at her again, just stared at her for the longest time. She glared at him and began to step back and away from him. When he slowly leaned toward her, it felt as if she was frozen in place, just waiting for him to kiss her.

His lips brushed against hers softly, then a second time. He pulled back slightly, tilting his head more, sliding his hand up to the back of her head, cupping it and pulling her forward and into his kiss. He kissed her gently at first, and then pulled her lower lip into his mouth to suckle it.

Suddenly, everything around her just dropped away—the sounds, the smells, everything seemed to fade away as he deepened the kiss. When his tongue slid along the seam of her lips, begging her for permission to enter, she let him in. As soon as her mouth opened slightly, his tongue darted forward to mingle with hers.

Pete had been kissed before, but nothing like this. Her whole body responded to him, to his mouth, his body. She hesitantly slid her tongue along his and felt his growl, felt it rumble from his chest she was pressed so tightly against. He suddenly pulled away, stepped back from her. She staggered again, only this time it was not from exhaustion but being tossed back by him. When he went to grab her, to keep her from falling, she stepped back further and snapped.

"Don't touch me! Don't you dare touch me again! Who the hell do you think you are? Are you enjoying this? Are you trying to drive me insane? Because I gotta tell you, you—" This time, it was she who growled and turned away.

Pete started to move toward the door to leave the bedroom, and he flashed in front of her again, this time to stop her. Again, she stepped back, but instead of backing away from him, she clasped her hands together, brought them around, and connected with his right jaw, snapping his head hard to the left. Then in a nasty move, brought her knee up and connected quite nicely with his groin and his manly parts. Her hands snapping against his jaw had hurt. There would be a bruise tomorrow, she thought. But the satisfying grunt coming from him made her think it was worth it.

She went into the hall and realized she was in the MacManus' house, and moved quickly to the front door. She saw Aaron step out of the kitchen so he was sure to intercept her just as she cleared the last step of the grand staircase. She was so not in the mood for him either and didn't say a word to him but kept moving toward her goal of out of this house.

"Pete, I'd like to have a few words with you while Dominic recovers, if you wouldn't mind?"

She didn't even think about how he knew the other man, Dominic, she supposed, was hurt.

"As a matter of fact, I do mind. Stay away from me. I don't want to have to hurt you either."

He either didn't listen or didn't think she'd follow through. But she was beyond being pissed and didn't stop to think about the fact that a full grown man, a vampire, was in her way. He was just there.

Without thinking about what she was going to do or slow down her forward motion, she swung her entire body around, landing on her hands just as her feet slammed into his chest. It was a nice trick she had learned from a guy she traded computer lessons for. He taught her how to fight dirty and she taught him how to use the Internet. Aaron flew across the living room and hit the far wall, knocking the wind out of him.

Another man—Christ, was everyone this man knew huge?—came out of the kitchen at full speed. He grabbed her around the waist, leaving her arms free. He will regret that soon enough, she thought with a smile. She twisted around in his arms, grabbed two handfuls of his long hair, and knocked her head into his nose, breaking it. When he loosened his grip enough, she broke free and brought her knee up and for the second time, she unmanned a vampire. She stepped over his inert body and out into the early morning.

She was nearly to the garage where she could see her bike parked when Sara cleared her throat behind her. Pete turned quickly and just managed to catch herself from harming the woman a few feet behind her.

~~~

Sara knew what had happened to each of the men. As soon as she felt Pete wake up, Sara got up herself thinking to go to her and thank her again. She had been standing just inside her bedroom door when she heard Dominic groan in pain. Reaching out to him, she realized what Pete had done and why, and smiled.

Following Pete down the stairs, a goodly distance behind her, she watched as Aaron had tried to stop her as well. That fancy footwork had Sara smile and wince. Aaron would be fine, but he would be mad. She had told him before that women, especially pissed off women, did not like to be cornered and were not rational either.

Colin must have felt Aaron's pain and came running out of the kitchen and got a broken nose for his trouble. Sara was still smiling when she walked out the door and saw that Pete was going to leave.

"You fight dirty. And mean. I like that. Going somewhere?" Pete seemed to relax a little, but Sara could tell that she was still wary. She was sure that Pete would not hit her, but she wasn't taking any chances and stayed five feet from her.

"He kissed me. The fucking bastard kissed me. He kissed me and then pushed me away like I had attacked him or something. This whole house is nuts, you're aware of that, aren't you? I've never...I'm leaving. Don't you dare try to stop me. I mean it, Mrs. MacManus. I'll hurt you as well."

Pete was crying and Sara's heart went out to the young woman. He had hurt her. He had not hurt her physically, but she still hurt deep inside. Sara wanted to take Pete into her arms and hold her, and then go in and kick some vampire ass.

"I'm not going to stop you, well, not really. But I did wonder if you knew that you are only dressed in a t-shirt and panties? I have no doubt that you can ride that monster without shoes. But I'm reasonably sure that once you get to your apartment, that Booger person and whoever else lives there will notice your lack of attire."

Pete looked down at her clothes, and then at the house. She began playing with the hem of the shirt. Sara realized that she had never seen that shirt before, that it must have belonged to Dominic. It was much too large to belong to the tiny woman who was wearing it. Pete took another quick look at the front door, and then looked back at Sara.

"He kissed me. Why did he do that? Why did he do it then toss me away? I'm not dirty and I...I didn't ask him to, didn't even want him to. I mean, it was nice. Very nice, but I didn't ask him to do it. I just wanted to go pee. Then I was going to leave."

"I have a good idea why he did it, but I'll let him explain that to you. Would you please come into the house and talk to him? Or we could just gather up some clothes and you can leave now. Okay?"

In a voice that was low, so low that another human might not have heard it, Pete said, "I don't even know his name and he kissed me."

Sara stiffened at that. To have a mate meant all sort of wonderful things to a couple, especially a vampire who was as old as Dominic. Sara knew that now that he had tasted her, touched her, he would only want more from Pete, need more from her. But to not even tell her who he was, or even to talk before kissing her was...Sara and Dominic had a lot to talk about, it seemed.

Sara led Pete into the house, and left her in the kitchen while she went to Dominic's room to gather Pete's clothes. Sara told the men that were recovering in the living room not to even think about confronting the woman in the kitchen. Or they would have to answer to her. And she left them in no doubt that she would not be as gentle as Pete had been.

"And you," pointing to Dominic, "don't even think about leaving this house. You and I are going to have a conversation and it won't go well for you if I have to go looking for you. And believe me, I will. I'm in no mood to fuck around anymore with you. You will be right here when I return or you'll be one sorry man. Do I make myself perfectly clear?"

"Yes, mistress."

Sara continued on up the stairs. She had just had twins and these people were making a mess of things. Well, no more.

After Pete left the house, Sara sat down with Dominic. She didn't want Aaron there, but he insisted that he was there purely for entertainment value, he told her. Dominic just glared at the vampire. For some reason she could not understand, that pissed her off more. She owed that woman her life and those of her children. It was time someone made him realize he could not toy with Pete as long as she was around, or he would have to answer to her.

"I want you to stay away from her. You brought her here against her will, you kissed her, and she doesn't even know your name. As your master's mistress and his mate, I demand that you stay away from her from now on. It is quite clear that you don't want her as your mate. You have made that perfectly clear from the moment you met her. Fine! Then don't go near her again. If you do, then I will make sure that you either regret it, which you know I can, or you'll mate with her — your choice. Have I made myself clear?"

"Perfectly. Is there anything else?"

She wasn't happy with his tone, but she would live with that. When she said that there was not, he got up and left. She looked over at Aaron who was smiling at her.

"Well done, my dear. Nothing like making someone want something they really need by telling them it's off limits to them. I'm impressed." She hoped he was right, hoped they were both right.

~~~

Pete showed up at the Mackey Corporation at seven-thirty that morning. She was going to be working for them for at least a week setting up their new payroll and accounting programs.

Mr. Mackey had contacted her a few days ago, telling her that he had had her investigated and had found nothing that would make him not want her to come in and work for them. He did tell her that a query around the computer shops and programmers in the neighborhood said she was not only the best in the field, but that she was the most trustworthy person around as well.

"I really appreciate your advice and the heads-up about Sailor. He was into the company for over six hundred thousand. It was a hard hit to the company, but I believe we are going to be able to get most of it back. He tended to spend his money locally and I'm getting his purchases, as it where. He is in jail for theft. I don't want this to happen again. I'd like for you to show us what you can do to prevent this from happening in the future."

Pete spent the next two days going through each program that they had and made a list of who had access to the files and how the information was obtained by a person. Some of the techs had both card reader access and password. Most of the other personnel had only password. And a majority of them had their passwords written down somewhere. A few even shared them with co-workers. In some cases, she found programs left running and email and payroll information up while the person went to lunch or the bathroom.

She had better computer skills than she had people skills so she stayed to herself during most of this time. The men in the office nearly fell all over themselves trying to get her attention and the women just tried to ignore her. But a woman as beautiful as her and as elusive just drew more attention.

Pete just didn't notice anything going on. Well, she did but chose to ignore it. She was so wrapped in what she was doing that she could have been alone in the entire building and it would have made the same impression on her. She liked staying busy. It kept her from thinking.

She and Mackey met on Thursday morning in his office. His daughter Shelia was there as well. Shelia had a pretty good head on her shoulders about the computer aspect of the business. She was no way near the level of Pete and they both knew it. They were comfortable with it. Shelia told Pete on Tuesday that she was glad to have her there and that her dad was finally coming into this century.

"How do you want this, Mr. Mackey? Straight up or honey coated? I can do either, but straight up will save me time trying to figure out how to say it nicely." She grinned at him.

"Straight up, Pete. I think I can take it." She hoped he could as well.

"You have a crappy set up to input your payroll. There are over seventy people who have access to the files that generate the final checks and over two hundred who can manipulate their own time sheets as late as the night before checks are printed. That has got to be a nightmare for your payroll department, by the way. There are, at the very minimum, eighty-four input errors on last week's timesheets alone, costing you a cool ten grand. I've already fixed the time sheets for this week's payroll and froze the account as of Tuesday morning. You also need a centralized accounting and a clock-in program, one that charges each person's work to the specific department. That is where you'll find most of your problems—double payroll when someone works in another department and charges their time to each one."

"Christ. Maybe I should have asked for it honey coated. How do I fix that? I'm sure you know a way one, right?"

Pete nodded. She liked Mr. Mackey. He was a straight up sort of guy and he didn't pull any punches either.

"Yes, I do. When a person signs onto his computer with his badge, they're on the clock and in the department they're working, same to sign off again. The program is inexpensive and easy to install. I can do that for you in less than two hours. The badges that you use already have the program installed. I just need to turn it on and set up the computer mainframe to recognize it. The other issue you have is your accounting department."

"Accounting? I thought we'd worked those out when you were here before. You mean there are things going on now, or something we missed?"

"The program is fine. It's your entire department. Were you aware that most of the time used in that department is online shopping, Internet usage not pertaining to work, Facebook, eBay and other sites that are costing you major downtime? About sixty-four percent of the day, as a matter of fact. If you take that service off their system grid, you can lower the percentage of people in that department alone by fifty-six percent with a payroll savings of four hundred thousand per year. Less people will also mean less mistakes and less access to your bank accounts. That will also make the department's productivity rise up to nearly ninety-six percent."

"Can't I just tell them not to use those sites unless they're on their breaks?" Mackey asked.

"You can ask until you're blue in the face, but the truth is, no one thinks they're using the Internet all that much. If you asked most of them, they would probably tell you they're only on it for a few minutes, when in actuality, they've been on it nearly their entire shift. No, I would remove the temptation."

Shelia was frantically writing notes, trying to keep up with her, so Pete reached into her backpack and handed her a copy of what she had found. She leaned back in her chair and waited.

"You found this all out in two days? Christ, I wonder what you could find if you were here for a month. I shudder to think how much more I'm losing daily in my other departments. I take it you have that program with you now and that you have a general idea who should be let go in the accounting department?" Mackey stood up and began pacing the room.

Pete bristled. Damn it, she had not asked to come here. He had asked her to find his mistakes. She'd had enough of people for awhile. As soon as she left here, she decided, she was becoming a hermit.

"Mr. Mackey, if you don't like what I've just told you, fine. No harm done, I'll just move on. I gave you the information you asked for. I don't give a rat's ass if you use it or trash it. Everything you need is right there in your daughter's file. If you'll both excuse me, I have another job." She had gathered up her pack and was nearly to the door when he stopped her.

"Wait, Miss Bartholomew, Pete. I'm a businessman and I have a business that you've just told me is losing money, not by my hand, but by employee theft. I didn't mean to imply what you are telling me is your fault. On the contrary. It's just that in the past two hours, you have torn apart my whole payroll system and told me I'm losing half a million a year paying my accounting department for shopping online. That's a lot to handle. I guess I needed it a little more honey coated than I thought. Please, Miss Bartholomew, come have a seat."

She came back into the office and continued to break apart each department one by one. The money he was losing and the profit he would make by following her suggestions was staggering. When he followed her plan and there really was no doubt he was going to follow everything to the letter, she thought, he would see a net profit of three million in the first year and a twenty-eight percent increase each year following that, she told him.

On Friday morning, Pete received her consulting check from the Mackey Corp. The amount on the check was well over what they had agreed upon. When she asked to see him about it, Shelia took her into her new office and explained that they had discussed her plans and what the company's profit and loss statement would look like once her suggestions were implemented, and the board had decided to pay her salary and a percentage of the profits they would net thanks to her.

"They were only being fair since you had found the money in the first place. We would have had to have paid a consulting firm had we brought them in. And Daddy is sure that they would not have found near the amount of mistakes that you did. Take the money, Miss Pete. You earned every penny of it."

Overwhelmed and slightly dazed, Pete left the offices.

She went to the bank that was holding the account open for the house being built by the Becca Foundation, the account set up to pay for Becca's Place and put half of the check, one million dollars of it, into the account. She then took out her list of people she helped out and she and the bank assistant put money into over sixty accounts, enough for some of these people to live on for a couple of months more without losing their houses, cars, or both, and with enough left over to pay the utilities and buy food within that time frame as well.

Most of the people she helped had no idea that a single person was helping them. It was just as well. Pete would have been thoroughly embarrassed to have them know. The bank assistant could lose her job if anyone got upset about Pete putting money into their accounts, but so far, no one had complained. The assistant manager had told her that she must notify each person who was helped and not to ever mention the donor's name. Everyone was happy about that arrangement, especially Pete.

CHAPTER TEN

"Miss Pete, it is I, Dunc. I was wondering if you could call me at the mansion as soon as you are free? I have a problem with one of the computers."

Pete listened to the message again and then re-read the handful of phone messages from the same phone number, and a few with a name she did not know. She didn't want to go back there. She didn't even want to call the number. She went to the payphone in the hall and waited for one of the other residents to get off then made the dreaded call.

"It's Pete, Dunc, what can I do for you?" It was nearly seven o'clock on Friday night, and she knew that the vampires would be awake soon if they were not already.

"Oh, miss, I was wondering if you could please come by and look at my kitchen computer? It will not...well, it will not do what I want it to. I have rebated it several times and I have unplugged it as well, but I'm having no luck."

"You rebooted it, Dunc, not rebated it, but I'll be over in about an hour. Is there anything else? I mean, I have a lot of messages here from someone named Dominic Marshall."

"Master Dominic stays here, miss. He is the man who brought you here when the babies were born. I do not know why he has been calling. Would you like me to ask him to stop?"

"No. No, I guess...he can call if he wants. Doesn't mean I'll return his call. Is he there now?" So that was his name.

She had thought of the kiss a lot over the past week. Her heartbeat would speed up at the thought of how he had claimed her mouth, devoured her really. His body pressing hard against hers made her nipples hard just to think about it. Then she would remember how he had pushed her away from him and she would be embarrassed all over again.

"No, miss, he has not been here for a couple of days now."

Pete wondered, not for the first time, how much the household knew about them and their tempestuous relationship. She had beaten up three large men when she had left the last time. She knew that if they had wanted to, any of them could have kept her there, but they had not wanted to hurt her and they would have too. Of this she had no doubt.

She and Duncan made arrangements for her to be there in an hour and hung up. She had gotten all her tools back from Toby and gathered them up to take with her. She was just putting them into her saddle bags when she felt the first touch.

They had found her. It would only be a matter of time now before they showed up, very little time before they tried to stake their claim again. She knew as soon as she had helped the babies they would come. Her family, they were coming for her. She went back into her little room and made sure there was nothing there she could not live without. She could not come back, not now, not without endangering the other people living there too. She found Booger and gave him her part of the rent for the next two months and left.

Pete showed up at the outer gate forty-five minutes later. She drove through and up the drive just as Dominic appeared in the kitchen. When she walked in the door and saw him, she nearly turned around and left. But he stepped toward her and stopped when she stiffened.

"I was wondering if I may talk with you after you fix Duncan's computer? Please?" he asked. He did not come any closer to her to, which she was both happy and upset about.

"All right, I suppose so. But you'll not touch me again. I don't even want you to come close to me. Understand?"

He agreed that he only wanted to talk. So she sat at the kitchen desk top and worked through what Duncan had done. To her surprise, it took her nearly two hours to muddle through the problem. It should have taken less time, but her mind kept drifting to the man in the other room. It was not until she pulled it away from the wall to check the connection that she noticed he had switched around the input cables. She switched them back and sat back while the machine rebooted. She looked at the man hovering about the kitchen with her.

"You know," Pete said, not looking at Duncan. "Once I agreed to talk to him, you could have told me what you had done to get me here. It would have saved everyone a few hours of waiting for me to find it."

"I'm sure I do not know what you are talking about, Miss Pete. But having someone stew in their own juices has never hurt anyone. And if I were a young lady such as you, I would not take any poop from him either," Duncan said with a snort.

Pete laughed and didn't even bother correcting him. She really liked Dunc and would certainly miss the odd little man. She waited until the computer finished its set up then went to find Dominic.

He was in the half room, so called because it was halfway between the living room and the dining room. When either of the two rooms needed extra space, the pocket doors could be slid into place, making the rooms appear to be one.

She walked in and stood near the doors. She was not sure what she was supposed to call him, or how to address him, so she did neither.

"You wanted to speak to me?"

"Yes, thank you for allowing me this time. I wanted to apologize to you for my behavior the other night. I...I don't have an excuse for the way I acted." He stayed seated. She looked around the large room and saw that they were alone.

"Are you telling me you're sorry for the way you acted or that you kissed me then pushed me away?" Leave it to me, she thought, to get to the heart of the matter. "Or is it because you kissed me at all? You know, it doesn't really matter. Thanks. I'll be going now." But she couldn't make herself walk away.

~~~

Dominic stared at her. She was really quite beautiful and he suddenly realized that he had never seen what color her eyes were. Sara had said they were unique, but he wanted to, no, he needed to see them for himself.

"Why do you wear sunglasses all the time?"

His question threw her off, he could tell. And he was just a little bit glad about it. She had thrown him off at least daily since the first time he saw her.

"They put people off. The color, I mean, it puts people off. They don't know what to do when they see them, so I wear the glasses to hide them. Plus, the light makes my eyes sore a little and sunlight can give me a migraine if I'm not too careful. Most people believe me to be weird anyway. This is just another thing for them to speculate on. You didn't answer me."

"No, I didn't. I'm not sure I want you to know my answer just yet. May I see them? I just realized that I have never seen your eyes." Dominic wanted to go to her, but he waited, waited for her to indicate that she would not bolt if he did. He wanted to touch her, feel her skin next to his again, but he didn't, for her.

She shrugged her shoulders as if to say, "What do I care? I warned you about them." He walked slowly across the room to her, and when he was less than a foot from her, he started to reach up and remove the glasses from her face. He looked down at her then and silently asked for permission to remove them. Instead of answering, she reached up and pulled them off, closing her eyes against the sudden brightness of the room as she did so.

When she opened them, Dominic slowly reached out and cupped both cheeks in his large hands and tilted her head at a better angle to the light. He studied her intently, moving her head this way and that to watch the light reflect off of the brilliant silver color. He looked down at her then, really looked at her face when her saw her tongue slip out from between her lips and lick them moist. And if that wasn't enough to make him groan, she worried her full lower lip with her teeth. He watched the whole process with great fascination.

"Are you satisfied?"

Her whispered innocent question brought an immediate response from his already hardened cock. He could tell her in a word just how unsatisfied he was at the moment, but could not make his throat work around the sudden dryness of this mouth. He wanted her with every fiber of his being.

And he was suddenly very glad he was holding her. He was sure that if he wasn't, she would leave him.

"Pete...Pete, tell me your name. Your real name, I mean. Mine is Dominic Patrick Marshall. I'm originally from England, old England."

"Why?" Her voice was husky and smooth. She licked her lips again. Her own body was responding to his closeness and he could smell her arousal. He watched her eyes become a darker shade of silver, more brilliant in their color as the moments passed and he touched her.

"Tell me, please. I need to know."

His answer was not very good, but as he had said it, he leaned forward and kissed the side of her mouth. A light kiss, small tastes of her as it were.

"It's...it's Piccadilly. Piccadilly Fresno. I want you to step back away from me. You...you're making me nervous. You have to...you need to...please, Dominic, I..."

"Yes, Piccadilly, I need it too. I very much need it too." His mouth brushed hers once more then he deepened it to a kiss.

His kiss demanded a response from her and he got it. There was no timid response from her this time or between them. With his hands still on her cheeks, he pressed her mouth open for his and tasted her. He captured her groan as it rumbled from deep and moved across his tongue like a taste, a taste like ambrosia. Dominic shifted her body to his left and used his right hand to cup her ass, tightening her hard against him. Lifting her feet up off of the floor, Dominic felt her pour over him.

Never had he felt this way about sex or a woman. No, he realized, not sex. This had moved beyond just sex. This was a claiming; he needed to claim her. Shifting her again, he ran his hands along her thighs and helped her wrap those incredible legs around him. He was not going to take her here for as much as he wanted to. He needed to make love to her in his lair, in his bed.

Dominic, with Pete wrapped around him, moved to the panel in the far wall that would take them to the lower levels and opened it. The trip took them longer because neither could stop touching, kissing exposed flesh, marveling at new tastes. He'd had to try several times to get his door to open because he kept losing his concentration on an otherwise easy task.

Finally, the door sprang open, and he pulled her close again and moved into the room. With a swift kick, the door slammed and locked behind them. He wanted to slow down; he wanted to rip her clothes off and take her while standing there. He wanted to taste her slowly, savor her body. He also wanted to sink his cock deep inside of her, fuck her until neither of them could stand. His body ached, his need was incredible.

"Piccadilly, I need you, baby. Tell me. Tell me that you need me as well. I want to hear you say it, tell me."

He cupped her breast through the shirt she had on and knew that she was bare beneath it. His already heated blood felt as though lava was racing along his veins, through him. He felt her arch into his palm, the nipple hard against his thumb. He bent down and took it into his mouth, nipping at it through the material, soaking it through.

When her approval of a hissed yes spilled from her mouth, Dominic felt as though he could take on the world. She pulled him closer to her breast by grabbing a handful of his hair and holding him there. Her hips began to move against his groin and his cock, making it difficult for him to think.

Dominic could smell her now. Her arousal was hot and heavy, making him crazy with need. He reached between them and yanked his shirt in half, buttons from the front flying all over the room. Hers was next. The thin material of her t-shirt didn't stand a chance against this primal need to be with her. This time, when he suckled at her breast, he tasted her skin, the heady taste that was unique to her.

He moved up her neck and along her jaw, nipping still and sucking on her hot skin. Her body was as on fire as his. He pulled her lower body from his and heard her whimper. He knew how she felt, but it would be worth the moment of separation as he pulled the snap open to her pants and slid the zipper down. She soon got the idea and began working the belt loose to get to his button as well. By the time he had managed to get his hands down the back of her pants and cupped her bare ass again, she had his pants undone and was stroking his cock through his briefs. The bed even at three feet away was too far. They would never make it, he thought with a grin. And if she kept touching him as she was now, he was not going to last much longer anyway.

Dropping to his knees before her, he stripped her off the rest of her clothing. Standing before him was the most magnificent sight he had ever had the pleasure of gazing upon.

He looked up at her and saw that her eyes had turned and were now glowing. His own eyes had turned as well. He could see her through the red haze of his heightened state of need. Running his hands up her legs to her thighs, he never stopped looking at her face as she spoke to him.

"We need to stop. I don't think this is a very good idea. I don't...I don't think I like you very much. And we...this is going way beyond us just talking."

"No, I don't think so. I'm going to taste you, love you with my mouth until you scream my name over and over." He flicked his finger up the seam of her nether lips. "Here, here is where I'm going to taste you." He could feel her heat. See the wetness gathering in the curls there. Slowly, he inserted his finger into her, stretching her, widening and separating his fingers as he pumped them in and out of her, into her heat and wetness. When she started to close her eyes, he stopped her.

"Pete, honey, watch me. Watch me as I stretch you for me. I'm going to bury my cock deep inside of you, feel you wrap around me. I'm going to ready your body for me. Then I'm going to fuck you, make you mine. Watch me."

When she focused again, he slowly inserted another finger deep into her again. He watched her, her body undulating up and down against his hand, her juices coating his fingers and hand.

"That's it, baby. Feel me inside you. Christ, you're so hot. And you're wet, so wet for me. I need to taste your cream."

Dominic pulled out his finger and stuck it into his mouth, moaning loudly at the honeyed taste of her. When he had licked and sucked his finger dry of her, he leaned forward and kissed her thighs, first one then the other. Her need was evident in her scent, her needy response to him and her body making him dizzy with an overwhelming need to claim.

He inserted his fingers again and leaned in to lick at her. His tongue joined his fingers and he fucked her with his mouth, never touching her clit until he was sure she was ready for him. He removed his fingers from her and pulled her thighs further apart, giving him more room to taste her. Just as he sucked her clit into his mouth and teased it with his tongue, he pumped harder into her, stroked her hard then softly over and over, flatting his tongue against her clit. He couldn't seem to get enough of her and wondered if he ever would.

She was so close; her cries and moans filled his head. He could feel her reaching her peak. He wanted to taste it, her first time. He needed to taste her come for him.

"Come for me, baby. Let go and come now." Her legs clamped down hard onto his head and she rode his mouth. When she came, she screamed, her body pulsing around his finger and mouth.

He lapped her tender flesh, bringing her to peak twice more as he did. He wanted her now. His cock was aching to be inside of her. He gently guided her to the floor. He leaned over her lax body and looked at her.

"I want you, baby. I want to be inside of you so badly I ache. I need to be inside of you."

Dominic moved up and between her legs. He kissed her tenderly and completely. He needed to slow down, he realized. His size and her virginity would be a painful combination for her first time. And he didn't want her to be marred by a painful memory.

"Please, Dominic, I need you. I want you inside of me, please." Her begging nearly tore him apart, but he knew she would love him more if he remained strong.

"I know, love, but I don't want to hurt you. We need to go slowly this time." He moved up, positioned his cock at the core of her, and moved slowly into her. He felt her stiffen beneath him and he stopped. "All right? Am I hurting you?" He knew at the moment if she asked him to stop, he would. At this moment, if she asked him to do anything, he would die giving it to her.

"No, you feel so good there. I want more. Please, give me more of you, all of you." She moved up to meet his downward push. He stopped when he met with her maidenhead. He looked down into her eyes and fell in love.

"You...this will hurt, baby. I'm so sorry." And he slammed forward, quick and hard into her. She jerked back against the bed when he broke through and she tried to get away from him.

"Shhhh, baby, it's all right. I'm so sorry, Pete. I promise you that I didn't mean to hurt you. I will never hurt you again. Shhhh. I have you."

He didn't move his body, afraid of hurting her more. He just held her tightly to him and cooed softly into her ear. He petted her, touched her tenderly, and gave her comfort. When he felt her relax again, he moved slowly back and into her again.

"Dominic, please."

He reached down and grasped her hip, then slipped his hand beneath her, cupping her ass and tilting her upward, allowing him to slide deeper into her. He felt her legs rise and encircle his thighs, pushing up against him with each downward stroke. He was close to coming. He could feel his balls rise and tighten against him. His fangs elongated, his need to taste her, to mark her, imminent.

"Pete, I want to taste you. I need to taste you now." He moved his mouth along her jaw, nipping. He found her pulse, suckled it into his mouth. He could feel the blood pounding through her jugular.

"Yes, Dominic, please take me. Take all of me."

He kissed her where he would bite her, licked the pulse again to take away most of the pain, and bit down. Her blood filled his mouth; her power and the power of her essences roared through him. He drew hard on her vein and came.

His climax reverberated through him, gripping him hard. He poured into her, deep and completely, touching her womb with each hard thrust. She rolled over the edge of completion with him, her body like a silken sheath, it held him. He felt her milking and pulling him deeper into her. When he was spent, he collapsed on top of her, barely able to roll to the side at the last second and pull her atop him as he went. He didn't so much fall asleep as he did drift into unconsciousness along with her.

CHAPTER ELEVEN

She heard him stir a little but not wake yet. She didn't want to face him, not yet at any rate. There were no windows here below the ground so she stared into the empty fire grate and waited until he woke up.

Over an hour later, she felt him touch her mind. She allowed him some of what she was. He had panicked slightly when he discovered she was no longer beside him and wanted to give him this one bit of comfort before she told him she had to leave.

"I'm going to have to leave here soon. It's not safe. They're almost here, my family. They'll come for me now that they've found where I am. I've been hiding from them for nearly nine years now, you see, not using the curse that I have. But there was no way I could let the baby die, so I led them here, led them to all of you. I'm sorry, so sorry about that. I...we shouldn't have had sex. I shouldn't have let you bite me, but it felt so good, wonderful really. Now I'll have to go, lead them away from you and the others. I have to keep you safe, all of you."

"Come here, Piccadilly. Come over here and tell me why you think you need to leave me now. And why you think

105

that leaving me is the best solution. Because I can't let you go, not now. I love you," he said.

"You can't love me. Not me. You...just a few days ago you were tossing me away from you. And now you profess to love me? It was great sex, Dominic, but that's all it can ever be."

"I was a fool. I know what you are to me. I knew when I...I can't live without you, Pete. Now that we've mated, I can't ever feed from another person. I will die without you."

"Why? Why would you do something like that? You don't even like me. I don't even...I didn't even know your name until a few days ago. We can't be a couple. I'll have sex with you until I leave, but I'm not staying."

He didn't say anything. Pete was sure he thought he could make her stay, but she couldn't. Maybe some other time, before her family, she might have thought...but it mattered little now. They were coming. She decided to tell him everything. Make him see why they could not be a couple. She didn't move, didn't so much as acknowledge him, but continued her story, starting at the beginning this time.

"I was four years old when it started. I only had six brothers then, three older, the other three younger than me. The six of them, me, and my mother, all one big happy family. I never knew who my father was. In fact, I don't remember there being any men in my mother's life other than my brothers. She called them 'her boys.' Then suddenly, this man showed up. I actually think he knew my older brother somehow, but I've never been sure. He promised them everything if they would just learn from him, let him develop their powers."

"Powers? Like yours?" Pete locked at him. "I know you have them. I can taste them in your blood and on your skin. Are your brother's the same as you?"

"No. They're different. I'm not like them on any level. They were horrible...are horrible men. My mother wasn't any better, of course, always encouraging them in their experiments. They would conduct tests of will and strength on others, humans, they called them, as if they didn't consider themselves that at all."

"You aren't. Not entirely. I'm not sure what you are, but you aren't fully human. Pete, come here, please? I need to touch you."

She knew if she did go to him, she'd be lost. Pete kept staring at the grate and thought about her family and why she had to leave.

"They'd lure people to the trailer where we lived by telling them that they were going to be paid. All they needed to do was cooperate with them for a little while. First they'd feed them drugged food to get them to cooperate, then tie them to the iron maiden they'd made specifically for their 'work,' they called it. The horrible things they would do to those people. All the while this man would stand over them, telling them where to cut, how deep, and then how to collect their blood and other things. Then they would cause such horrific pain, slicing into them with their powers, cutting into their bodies with lightning or whatever their special talent was.

"One of them, Herne, would use his hands that he could morph into claws with razor-like talons. He practiced lengthening them, cutting deeper into those poor people as they lay there helpless, testing and practicing his ability to control it. The screams would ring through the trailer for days until they finally just died. The stronger they got, the more the man would come around. Almost daily toward the end of me living there. I think he is the main reason I left. He terrified me."

"Do you know who he was? Could he have been your father? Theirs maybe? It would help me to understand why you think you can't stay here to know what you've been fighting."

"His name was Sherman. If he had a last name, I'd never heard it. I don't think he was our father. He was too...too enamored of what they could do, surprised at how much they could show him." She sifted in her chair again. "I couldn't save them, any of them. I did try to once. I released a man, helped him out into the woods and gave him food and water. That man, Sherman, captured him the next day and brought him back. My brothers tied me to the wall and made me watch while they tortured the poor man, each one of them taking a turn to make him suffer unbelievable pain. When either of us would black out, they would stop and when we woke again, they would start all over. It took him a week to die. A whole week and because I thought I could help him. He was cursing me in the end, damning me and them for making him suffer. Sherman thought it was the greatest thing in the world and told my brothers that I should be rewarded for what I had done for them."

Pete heard Dominic curse. She was hurt by that. He was finally realizing that she was trouble that he would be better off by letting her go. Yeah, she hurt badly, but continued.

"When I hit puberty, things changed drastically for me. I had my first period at twelve and began to change physically, breasts, hips — womanly stuff. That's when the mark began to grow and shape itself to me. It was only a small leaf at first. I'd noticed it on my left hip when I was about six, I guess. It started at my thigh and grew up my back and along my spine. I could feel it as it moved, grew. By the time I was fourteen, I was fully marred by this thing. I tried to hide it and did a pretty good job of it too, but when it encircled my bicep and curled up and around my left ear, I couldn't anymore. When I turned sixteen, Sherman noticed it. I had almost convinced the others it was a tattoo that I'd had put there, but Sherman told them I was marked by a being too strong to allow my freedom."

She heard him shift again. She had turned in the chair in a way that she could no longer see the bed. When he came up beside her and scooped her up into his arms, she screamed.

"When I say I want to hold you, I want to hold you. Tell me this story, Piccadilly. Tell me so that I can show you how much I can protect you, how much I can love you. Why did Sherman want you to not be allowed freedom anymore?"

"He'd seen it move, see. He had seen it as it shifted along my body. When he asked my mom about it, she told him that the person whom she'd mated with had the same mark. She didn't know what he'd been, just as she didn't know who the fathers of the boys were. She had told him that she liked sex and that any man would do. She and Sherman were so proud of my progress; she'd said that she would do whatever he wanted. Then matters got worse, and I needed to leave."

"Tell me, love. I'm here. Tell me how matters got worse. And Piccadilly, you aren't leaving me and I'm not leaving you. No matter what is going on in your head right now."

"That summer, they decided to create a child with me. They had this monthly chart made up of my cycle and circled in red when would be the optimum time to have sex with me. And this would continue until one of them impregnated me. They were my brothers, and you know whose idea it was? My own mother. I shut the door to the mark and ran away. Sherman said that I couldn't hide from him. That he would find me no matter what. I was safe until the other day, when I opened the door for the little boy. But you understand, I couldn't let him die, don't you? Now I need to go." She didn't move yet. She really did not have the energy.

"Of course I do. You're mine and I protect what's mine. But I need to know how you feel them, how you know where they are? And how close are they?"

She thought he would be repulsed at the idea of her magic, or curse, as she called it, but he seemed more...concerned than mad. She did not understand him.

"Their magic, or whatever it is, speaks to me. I think it's because we all have the same mother maybe. I don't know. It's like I can feel their taint, taste it almost." She looked away and shrugged. Her tears threatened to spill.

~~~

"I didn't see it, your mark. Where is it, baby?" Dominic asked her quietly.

He was holding her tight now, close to him, and when he shifted and stood up, she did as well and faced him. She had wrapped a sheet around her body and she dropped it. There was a gentle stirring in the air, a small hum of magic then he felt it when she dropped the hold on herself and turned around to face him and let him see her fully for the first time.

Her eyes were glowing again, brightly this time, lighting the room as well as herself. The vine did indeed start at her thigh and wrapped around it and moved up her hip. She turned around so he could see her spine where it was growing up it as if her bone were a trellis, drooping here and there from the weight of the leaves. A single vine broke off from the mass and curled up her hair line and across her jaw to come up her cheek to her ear and curve below her left eye.

110

Yet another vine ran along her shoulder and down her arm to her bicep, once again wrapping around the muscle with a small curl drooping to her elbow and midway down her forearm. The vine was an intricate and beautiful work of art, and looked as real as anything ever seen in nature. The vines were dark greens and browns, as big as a thumb. The leaves were large and open with varying shades of green. But it was the flora that grabbed one's attention. There were hundreds of flowers in different stages of bloom, all in shades of reds, yellows, pinks and blues. The opened flowers were as big as a fist; the buds were as long and as thick as Dominic's thumb.

Dominic reached out to touch her, and was surprised to find heat coming from the vine and flowers even before he made physical contact with her skin. He spread his hand along her spine and the leaves moved, disturbed by his touch, he realized. He bent down to smell one of the flowers and the sweet scent of nutmeg and cinnamon wafted to his nose. He jerked back in surprise.

"Christ! It's your scent. I smelled it that first night. You smelled of cinnamon. I tried to blame it on the pantry, but it was your mark."

She started to step away from him, but he wrapped his arm around her waist and pulled her to him. He cradled her under his chin and held her. "No, Piccadilly. Not again. You're mine, I told you. Let me hold you. I need to hold you, baby."

He was awed at what she had shown him, and wanted to just keep her there close to his heart and with him to protect her. He scooped her into his arms and carried her to the bed where he laid her down and joined her. He covered them both with the comforter and pulled her closer still to him. He could feel her crying, the soft sniffle and the stiff way she was holding her body. He held her, whispering in her ear, kissing and soothing her as best he could until he felt her relax and fall into a fitful sleep.

Dominic did not sleep, but mentally reached out to Aaron and Sara and the other magical women in the Kiss. He told them what he knew, her name, her family's discovery of her and of the vines and their movement when touched. Everything she had shared with him. Mel was going to contact her other relatives, Shade was going to contact her mother, the Queen of Forest, Fiona. They would meet with Piccadilly in the kitchen in a few hours' time. They were all willing to work with her and for her. Then he told them about Sherman.

"I don't know a lot about him from before. But from the way she talked about him, I'm sure it's the same man from the cave when Shade had been hurt," Dominic told Sara and Aaron.

"Yes, I believe you're right. Dominic, did he...had he touched her, sexually?" Sara asked him.

"No, my lady, he did not. Nor will he ever. None of them will, not ever again, I assure you. She is mine. I have claimed her and we have mated. She thinks to leave me, to leave to protect us from him and the others. I can't let that happen. She's mine and I mean to protect her."

"Well of course she's yours. And we'll all protect her. She is as much our family as you are, Dominic. Let us get to work on this and we'll see you at last light. And Dominic, don't let her out of your sight. She is a crafty little thing."

Dominic grinned at the warning from Aaron. They both had taken quite a beating the last time she tried to get away from them, one he did not think either of them would forget.

Aaron was impressed with the young woman's courage and strength, he'd told Dominic when Dominic begged him for his help to protect his mate. And Aaron told Dominic that he could do no less than to help her, because — and none of them were under any delusions that it was anything but her — had it not been for Pete and her magic, the children would not be here.

Two hours before sunrise, Dominic woke Pete up. He dreaded telling her what he had done. Knew the only way to fight against evil was to combat it with all you had at your fingertips. With a power base of the magnitude he knew Sara's family had, he had no doubt that they would triumph against whatever forces Pete's family thought they had.

"Baby, I need you to wake up. I want you to meet with some people, my friends, our friends. They can help us, help you. Come on." She rolled over and snuggled deeper into his, no, their bed.

He kissed her along her shoulder and then rubbed his hand down her spine toward her firm ass. Need rumbled through him.

"Piccadilly, I told them all about your family. Aaron is expecting us upstairs soon."

Her eyes opened wide in surprise. "Dominic, what have you done? They'll think I'm a freak. I need to leave before my family gets here. I can't involve your friends in this. My family is a bunch of evil men, and my mother is too, as well as a whore. And Sherman is powerful and I believe him to be a tad off his rocker. I have to go." Pete jumped up and was rushing around the room looking for clothing.

Unfortunately, or fortunately depending on how one looked at it, he had torn most of her clothes from her last night, and they were in tatters all over the room.

"Pete, have you any idea what people would say if you told them your lover and mate is a vampire, that one of your friends is the cousin of the Queen of Magic? That Aaron, our master, is a vampire, and the friend of a pack of werewolves? Honey, freak left the building when Elvis did. These are our friends and they want to help us," he said.

He was distracted by her nakedness and every time she bent over to pick up another button, he nearly groaned out loud. She was just straightening up when she caught him looking at her ass. Putting her hand on her hip, she turned to glare at him. He finally lifted his gaze to her face and grinned at her.

"What do you think you're doing just lying there? We've made a mess of this room and I need you to help me get dressed," she demanded.

"No. Not yet."

He was suddenly standing next to her and behind her. He was as naked as she was. He pushed his cock against her ass and cupped her breasts as he stood behind her. He began pulling and tugging at her nipples, which had hardened to stiff peaks the moment he touched her. He could smell her instant arousal. His cock hardened incredibly harder.

"Lean into the chair. Put your hands on the back of it for me."

When she moved forward to do as he asked and she realized what he was going to do, her body wept for him.

"That's it, baby; now spread your legs wide for me. I'm going to fuck you like this. Take you from behind and make you come. Are you sore? I can...I will try not to be so rough, but I need to be deep inside of you."

She moaned when he leaned in to nip at her ass cheek, just breaking the skin and then licking the tiny wound closed. Being this close to her heat, it was all he could do not to drop to his knees and taste her again, suckle from her pussy until he had his fill of her. Standing, he bent his knees slightly and slowly entered her from behind, moving into her wet, hot pussy, and stopped. His body was so close to spilling inside of her he needed a moment to gather himself.

"Dominic, if you don't move inside of me, I'm going to hurt you. You know I can, too."

Her voice was husky with her need. Heat from her surrounded his cock and his balls tightened up closer to his body. He put his hands on her hips and moved deeper within her.

When he was seated fully inside her, he began to slide in and out, gripping her hips hard. There would be a mark, a deep bruise, but he did not care. He was mesmerized by the slickness of his cock as it moved in and out of her, wet with her cream and hard for her body. His need to mark her, to fill her with his seed, was paramount to anything else at the moment and he moaned at the thought of shooting his cum deep into her womb. He shifted to his left slightly and watched her breast jerk with each slam of his cock into her.

"Oh, Christ, Piccadilly, you're so tight. Every time you bent over to pick something up, it was all I could do not to come all over myself. But this is so much better. Slamming deep in you. I love being buried deep in this pussy. Soon, love, I'm going to fuck this sweet ass of yours. I'm going to fuck you here until you scream."

He stuck his thumb in his mouth to wet it and pressed it hard against her tiny rose. When her body jerked tight against his, he nearly lost his control. His movements became frantic as his need to come and bring her to with him moved over him.

"Please, Dominic. Harder. Fuck me harder. I'm so close, so very close. I want to feel your cum inside me. Now, please, now!"

He started slamming into her, hard and fast. Each time he slammed deep, he would feel her sheath pull him tighter.

When she stood up, leaned into his chest, bringing her hands up to his neck, he cupped her breasts and pulled hard on her taut nipples. He suddenly needed more and pulled from her. He jerked her around to face him, picked her up by her ass, slammed her against the wall, and entered her again just as she wrapped her legs tightly around his hips. Pete wrapped her hand around the back of his head, grabbed a handful of his hair, and yanked his head back, exposing his throat.

"Bite me! Fuck, Pete, bite me hard!"

She sank her teeth hard into his throat right where the pulse was pounding as hard as he was into her. She broke his skin and marked him with her bite, bruising the tender flesh. Dominic felt his blood fill her mouth. He jerked his head forward, pulling his own hair, and bit her at the closest place he could sink his teeth. Their release roared through them, their mutual climax nearly violent.

CHAPTER TWELVE

Pete took her shower first, not allowing Dominic to take one with her or she said they would never leave the room. He really didn't think that was such a bad plan, he told her. He could very well stay in this room with her for a few hundred centuries, but the others were waiting on them.

Dominic gave her one of his shirts to wear, but there was nothing they could do about her panties so she ended up in a pair of his boxer briefs. They were miles too big for her. He seemed to take special pride in that, because of him, she had no underclothes. She continued to glare at him every time he grinned at her.

When they walked into the kitchen, everyone turned to them. Pete, as she had asked him to call her around the others for now, stepped behind Dominic to hide from the group gathered there. Dominic simply reached behind him, pulled her into the front of him, and kissed her hard on her neck.

Dominic looked directly at Aaron and said to the room in general, "I've...we've mated and bonded. She is my mate. As my master, I ask for your blessings."

A mated vampire couple, Dominic had explained when she had asked, meant that they had only had sex. Couples could and did live for centuries like that, never taking blood from the other. The non-vampire of them, most of the time a human, would never age, but they could die if mortally injured. The blood exchange was what bonded them both mentally and physically, and also made them both vampires.

"Welcome to my Kiss, Piccadilly Fresno Bartholomew." Aaron stood and embraced Pete with a kiss to each cheek. Aaron then did the same with Dominic.

Pete glared at Aaron first, then at Dominic. Dominic flushed and glared at Aaron as well.

"Don't be mad at Aaron. He means well. He needed as many details about you as he could get...I told him everything so he could get as much information about your family as he could. I didn't know he was going to blab it to everyone and his brother."

She was embarrassed, not mad at him. Dominic seemed to realize this, kissed her quickly on her nose, and grinned like a loon. She so wanted to smack him silly.

"Poo on them, all men can be such asses sometimes. I think it's a perfectly lovely name. Come now, meet the rest of your new family, dear. I'm Elizabeth; this is my mate Phillip. We're Mel's and Sara's grandparents. Sara is our son's daughter, who is no longer with us. This is Savannah and James, they are Mel's parents and Savannah is our daughter. Colin and Shade you have met. Duncan is the nicest man I've ever known, but he claims that he knows you best of all. This is Penny. She is the most wonderful cook. Speaking of which, you must be starved. Let's get you some food while we talk."

They had to adjourn to the dining room as the women had to eat. When Duncan set a large plate of food in front of her, she looked up at him. He just winked at her and said, "Its home cooked, miss, just for you."

It took her several seconds to realize he was referring to the conversation that they'd had once when she was installing the computer for him.

Pete toyed with the amazing amount of food that was before her. It wasn't until Dominic whispered in her ear that if they continued for an eternity like they had just before they left his lair, she would need to keep up her strength. She could do that by eating her breakfast. Aaron laughed at that and when he had chanced a glance at his own mate, he sobered up quickly. Sara had the most deceptively sweet look on her face.

After ten minutes of eating and joking around as a tight family would do, they got down to business. Dominic reached over and picked Pete up and sat her on his lap. The squeak from her sent the entire room into giggles.

"Your family is indeed on their way here, Piccadilly. According to the information I got earlier this morning, they left on Sunday morning, just after you helped to bring my children safely into the world," Aaron explained after they were seated around the large room.

"I know that I've drawn them here by helping you and your family, Mr. MacManus, and I've also told Dominic I will lure them away from your family as soon as possible. They are a dangerous bunch and I won't have them brought to your family."

"You've no idea how dangerous a vampire can be when it comes to what is his. So there will be no more nonsense about you leaving. Now, as I was saying, you now have seven brothers, and your 'mother,' for lack of a better term, is traveling with them. There was no sign of Sherman when they were seen last. But he could be traveling by other means. The Bartholomew's might arrive sometime late day after tomorrow — I absolutely refuse to call them your family.

However, I've arranged a couple of detours and 'accidents' to befall them, which should give us a day or two more."

"Accidents." Pete looked at Aaron and grinned. "I'll just bet you have. What do you have, some sort of vampire smoke signals that you watch? And it alerts you when they are coming closer?"

"Don't be impertinent. I have favors owed to me. And that, my dear, is all you are going to know about that."

For some reason, his statement, though said with a smile, sent chills down her spine. Pete decided that keeping an eye on him might be a good idea. Aaron MacManus was a very terrifying individual.

"Why don't you just stop them altogether? Why just slow them down? I don't understand," Phillip asked, concern lacing is voice.

"Because they won't stop until they have me. One or all of them will keep coming until they get what they want or they're stopped permanently. There's something else you should know. I'm not...I can't...this curse; it won't stay down shut down now. I'm...I'm barely able to hold it closed as it is. It's like a beacon and that is what is leading them here. And I can feel the stupid magic getting stronger too," Pete said.

"Since when? I mean, when did you start to lose control over it?" James knew a lot about magic, Dominic had told her. Just after he had become mated to Savannah, he'd started keeping a journal of sorts.

He had started out just keeping notes on them, then pictures he had drawn of the beings he'd had contact with or found. He had a journal for each type of being he had learned about. Phillip was thumbing through one now. It was a very plain notebook and the writing in it was with, of all things, a quill and ink.

"After we, hummm, we had sex, then...when he...I bit him, you see, and well, I bit him hard. I...that is to say, I tasted him, his blood. I bit him and tasted his blood, drank from him."

Even in her embarrassment, she was defiant. Even she knew it. She looked around the room as if to dare anyone to comment on her behavior. Of course no one did. Dominic, as her true mate, felt her emotions and hugged her body close to his, offering comfort and support through their bond.

"Show them, love. Let it go and show them your mark. I'm here for you. We are all here for you. Not one person in this room will be offended by it," Dominic said with an encouraging nod to her.

"I can show you most of it. But I won't strip down for you. There are limits to what even I will do in the name of keeping you safe, and baring my ass for the room so isn't one of them."

The room full of people laughed as she stood and pulled her shirt up in the back, and Dominic stood in front of her and hid her breasts from view.

"Could you pull your pants down to your knees, lass? Your under garment would cover your...well, it should cover you well enough, I believe," Colin suggested mildly.

Dominic's laughter quickly turned into a hard cough when Pete turned to glare daggers at him. She never stopped glaring as she answered Colin.

"I'm afraid that's not possible, Mr. Larimore. My panties, along with my shirt, seem to have been destroyed. It's a good thing that sort of opportunity will never happen again, isn't it, Dominic?"

"Ah, love, that's not fair! Besides, I'm sure we could buy a few extras just in case it happens again."

Pete had never wanted to smack someone so badly in her entire life as she did Dominic right then. And how the hell he got his eyebrows to wiggle like that was beyond her. Stupid man.

"Come with me, Pete. We'll have a look at my closet. I'm sure I have some things we can cover you with. We'll be right back." Sara reached out and the two of them headed for the stairs.

Pete was beginning to think she would never be anything but embarrassed around these people again. Not only was she expected to bare all, but to do so in front of strangers too. She trailed along behind Sara to the upper floors.

Shade came up with them. When Sara opened her closet doors after they had meet in her room, Pete could only stare open-mouthed. "Shit!" she said, then looked at Sara in horror.

"I agree, actually. I've gone overboard with shopping, but it's so much fun, especially when we all get together. And if you think this is bad, you should see Shade's closet. I'm not sure mine is even half that one. And believe it or not, Aaron is worse than I am." Sara stepped into the showroom sized closet and emerged a few minutes later with her hands full of clothes.

"Here we go. Now, I think I have a shirt that would be large enough for you to lift and cover yourself at the same time." Pete ended up with a sports bra and a pair of loose trainer pants with a pair of boxer briefs for women.

"Has Dominic bitten you yet? I mean, your mark, has he bitten your mark yet?"

Shade asked, startling Pete out of her wonderment of all the shoes Sara had. She was thinking, *Why you would anyone need more than one or two pair at a time?*

"I don't think so. It...we get sort of...sort of, and you know...it's very overwhelming while we...I don't think so." *Sheesh, did these people never get embarrassed?* she thought. She'd had sex for the first time in her life and it seemed everyone wanted some kind of detail about it.

"When Colin bit into mine, he received my powers. His aren't as strong as mine yet, but he's getting really good with them. I just wondered if the same could happen to you. I'm sorry; I didn't mean to embarrass you. But I know what you mean about it being overwhelming. But, damn isn't it wonderful!"

Pete had to agree—wonderful, overwhelming, spectacular, earth-shattering, mind blowing...oh yeah, it was all that and more.

"I was actually hoping that person from the restaurant, Queenie, could take them away. My curse, that is. I've never wanted it and I would like it gone. Maybe if it's gone, they'll stop looking for me." She glanced across the room and felt rather than saw Mel before she was clear and speaking.

"No, I can't. And even if I could, I wouldn't. You are fated to have those powers and I don't mess with those women, the Fates, I mean. Frankly, they scare the crap out of me." Mel shimmered in the spot even as Pete watched.

"They're not powers, but a curse. I don't want them. I've never wanted them. If you had to live with them, you'd think so too. They've done nothing but cause problems, and now look. Because of it, my family is coming here, and will stop at nothing to get me, including destroying every one of you. I'm not going back with them. I'll die first, I swear it. They're evil and...and I'm not, damn it."

Pete felt the vine move against her skin and across her back; the vine around her bicep tightened and pulled hard on her skin. Concentrating on her breathing and slowing her heart rate down, she was also able to slow down the movement of it somewhat. It was getting harder to keep the lid shut on it. The energy was surging now, the waves getting stronger with every breath she took. It was practically pulsing to be released from her hold on it. It was also beginning to scare her a little.

"And you won't, not as long as I'm still breathing, and I plan to do that for a very, very long time. Also, I think I can speak for everyone in this household when I assure you no one here thinks you're the least bit evil. You were there to save my children, Piccadilly. There's no telling what else the Sisters Three have in store for you, but until we know, you are our family and no one is taking you away from us," Sara said with conviction.

"Why? Why would you give two shits about me? Sure, I helped you with your kids, but they're safe now. I would think that you'd want me to move on and out of your hair. I would."

"One time I said the same thing to the big guy downstairs. I went so far as to ask him to end my life as I knew it. He did, though not the way I had hoped or asked him to. Now I have two children and him. And I have a family, one I didn't know I had. I would also be honored if you'd allow me to call you friend. You need to trust me, trust us."

Pete didn't say anything. She couldn't even if she wanted to. There was a large lump in her throat and she couldn't seem to get past it.

When they returned to the main level of the mansion, the others had gathered in the huge living room. As soon as Pete stepped over the threshold, Dominic was at her side.

She could see the concern in his eyes and had only meant to give him a quick peck on the cheek. As soon as her mouth touched his skin, need for him slammed into her. The tiny peck became a nip, the nip a bite, the bite a devouring kiss. Heat flared within her in an instant. It wasn't until someone cleared their throat that she realized where they were.

"I'm sorry. I...we..." She looked helplessly at Dominic. He just grinned at her, the arrogant ass. Pete wondered how she was going to stand the next five minutes with this man much less the next few years.

"No need to explain, lass. We've all been there. Why, I remember once I thought we'd have to turn away twelve hundred vamps so that Sara and Aaron could...how did you put it Dominic? Ah yeah, fuck like bunnies," Colin told her with a wink.

"That's quite enough out of you. I could tell her a few stories of the two of you as well. Like the time you nearly blew the roof off the house when you came. My ears rang for a month, I think," Aaron countered with a grin.

"Okay, gentlemen, moving on. Are you ready, sweetheart?"

Pete looked at Elizabeth and decided she really liked this woman. "I guess I'm as ready as I'll ever be." But before she could drop her tedious hold on it, James spoke up.

"Wait! Take off your glasses, please. I want to see your eyes when you drop your shields. Dominic said that they glowed. It could have some bearing on what you are."

"It seems Dominic was a busy, busy boy while I slept, wasn't he?" But she did as James had asked. "Ready or not, here I come." And she dropped her hold.

CHAPTER THIRTEEN

The room seemed to expand with the weight of her power; the walls seemed stretch and then recede. Pete's eyes glowed brightly at first then seemed to dim as her powers dissipated throughout the room. She was power.

"By all that's holy!" Phillip exclaimed loudly.

"Phillip? What is it? What's going on?" Elizabeth rushed to his side, fear for him evident in her voice.

Instead of answering her, he stood and walked to the young woman.

"It's...it's amazing. You're beautiful, my dear, absolutely breathtakingly beautiful. Let me see you, all of you, please?" He twirled his finger around, showing her that he wanted her to turn around fully for him.

Pete turned around slowly for him. She was standing there clad only in her borrowed bra and panties, but even she could tell that her mark was not the same as it had been yesterday, not even like it had been just hours ago.

"It's different from this morning, it's bigger, greener. The vines are thicker and there's...Christ, there are flowers now." Dominic had come to stand beside Phillip, just behind her.

"How? Tell me what else is different about it. Every detail you can remember, leave nothing out."

Pete watched as James pulled out his note pad and began making notes or something on it. I'm going to have to introduce him to the laptop, she thought vaguely. Her mind was not exactly functioning on all cylinders, it seemed.

"It's bigger on her back, wider," Dominic said. "Before it was just up her spine, like it was using it as a trellis. Now...well, now it's fuller, denser, I guess you could say. There are more flowers and buds as well, and the colors are brighter and sharper in appearance. They were bright before, but they glow now. There was just one vine going across her shoulder here, but now look. It drapes down and covers her entire shoulder down to her elbow."

"Dominic?"

She sounded scared even to herself, but she couldn't seem help it. She was terrified. She had never needed anyone in her life before. Now all she wanted was this man to hold her, to just touch her.

"I'm here for you, love. I'm not leaving you, not ever." He must have sensed her need for contact and reached out and took her hand into his, lacing their fingers.

"Mel, do you have your shields up full? All of you, I want you to drop your shields. All at once now — three, two, one, now!"

Phillip backed a few steps away from her even as he counted down. This was not helping, she thought.

Pete stiffened at the surge of power, and then she felt the mark, the sigil, as James had told her it was called, move and grow again. Dominic must have sensed something and squeezed her hand again. She suddenly needed more; she turned around and wrapped her arms around his waist. The others in the room looked at her in near silence.

~~~

"Dominic, touch her back please, gently. I want to see it move when you touch it. Then, when I tell you, I want you to press into the vines," Phillip said.

Dominic did as he asked and he felt the vine move and sway again as it had done in the bedroom, just as if it were a living thing. When he pressed his fingers into it the vine, it swallowed his fingertips. He watched as it seemingly swallowed his hands deep within its greenery.

"Pete, darling, may I try something, please? I'd like to try and hurt you. Could I try that, please? It's just a thought, but maybe it..." Phillip looked up at Dominic and saw alarm clearly written all over his face. He backed up another step and away from the two of them.

The deep rumbling sound coming from him was dark and dangerous. This was his mate, his true love. No one was going to harm her, not while he was still able to protect her.

"I won't hurt her, Dominic. I said I'd try to hurt her. I don't believe the vine is going to let me cause her any harm anyway. May I please continue? It's very important or I wouldn't ask. I know the value of a mate."

Phillip was a true immortal and could not be killed. Dominic knew this. But pain was friggin' pain no matter what kind of being one was. And there was no doubt that Dominic would hurt him badly if harm came to his love.

At Dominic's nod, Phillip drew back to ask for a knife. Sara handed him a blade of hers, but he switched to another because the one Shade had handed him was not of pure silver, nor was it magically enhanced. Phillip had an idea and excitement was clearly written all over his face. Dominic thought Phillip had an idea what, if not who, Pete was.

"Phillip, be careful. I don't want to have to kill anyone to save your sorry ass," Aaron said.

Dominic knew without a doubt that he would not be the only one to attack Phillip if his theory proved incorrect. There was an entire room full of beings, Aaron included, that would jump to Pete's defense if need be.

Phillip looked up at Dominic. Taking a deep, calming breath, he made to stab at Pete's back. But before it came within a foot of her, a vine lashed out and knocked the blade from his hand. Another reached out, wrapped itself around Phillip's throat, and lifted him from the floor a good two feet.

"Mother fuck!" Aaron said, and rushed forward.

Dominic started to push Pete behind him and to...to do what? He wasn't sure what the hell he was supposed to do to help. It was alive and, fuck, it was protecting her.

Dominic felt Phillip whisper through his mind. "Tell her to relax; no one is going to hurt her. She's a little frightened, poor thing. But for God's sake, don't let anyone touch her! Tell her, Dominic, comfort her. You're the key to this."

"Pete, honey, I need you to relax. No one is going to harm you, but if you'd like to kill this old fool, I'll gladly help you. The next time someone asks me if he can try to cut you, I'll castrate him for you. He thinks you're frightened. Like brandishing a knife at your back wouldn't scare most people. That's it, Piccadilly Fresno, relax, sweetheart." He was anything but calm, but he thought he sounded okay.

"I hate that name, you know. Making jokes, you're making jokes at a time like this! I'm not frightened one bit. But I may just have to kill one or both of you before this is over. Now, stop calling me stupid pet names or I swear to you, Dominic Marshall, I will stake you in your sleep. I'm not kidding either. I think you're all fucking nuts." Dominic could hear her relief in her voice, and her fear. The vine dropped Phillip unceremoniously onto the floor and curled around Pete again.

Aaron laughed and bent over in his own relief. The vine had not hurt Phillip and Pete was yelling at him. Just like old times, Dominic thought. This whole fucking house was nuts.

"Ah, Piccadilly, I think you will suit well in this family. And I do believe I'm getting much too old for this," Aaron said.

Dominic thought he may be as well. The reality hit him then and he broke down. Everything hit him at once. Pete being his mate, Phillip trying to hurt her, the flipping vine fighting back. It was suddenly just too much.

"Are you fucking out of your mind? Did you know that was going to happen? Jesus H. Christ! You dumb, stupid son-of-a-bitch, you scared the hell out of me. Don't you ever do that again, do you hear me?" Dominic snapped at Phillip.

"Just as I thought. Look, Dominic, the vine wasn't reacting to Pete's feelings at all. It was reacting to yours, Dominic, and your need to protect her. It's protecting you both," Phillip said with a grin.

The vine had begun to cover them both, everywhere Dominic was touching Pete skin to skin or through clothing, it didn't seem to matter, the vine enveloped them.

"Piccadilly, love, I know what you are. You, my dear, are a wood nymph," Phillip said with a huge grin.

Chapter Fourteen

"A wood nymph? I don't understand. Aren't they like fairies or something?" Pete was trying to absorb this, but it was difficult.

So much had happened in the past few days that she was having trouble focusing on anything for more than a few minutes. And these people, this man, was telling her she wasn't even human. Pete decided she really needed to have a quiet moment or a stiff drink. Maybe both.

"Actually, most nymphs are identified only through their magic. There are some nymphs who give life to the seeds in the ground, others who touch the flowers in the morning to bring them dew, thus giving them their first drink of water. Then there are the ones who are called water nymphs who help with the breeding and birth of all underwater life. They are mostly always female and nature spirited. Now you, you were a puzzle. Your mother is most likely a nymph herself. It is thought that when a nymph wants to mate, to breed as it were, she need only look deeply in the eyes of her intended victim and he wouldn't have any control over himself other than an uncontrollable need to mate. She must have bred with another nymph's mate because you said there were no other males in her life but your brothers. Nymphs, especially wood nymphs are extremely protective of their young. And you were born." Phillip read from his notes, so he missed her angry stance.

"Just like that! She's horny, finds another woman's mate, fucks him, and poof, here I am," Pete snarled.

"Actually, pretty much just like that, only you forgot that she would be ovulating too. That would be important, you see, for the fertilization process to work. I think there might be a cycle chart somewhere in my notes at home. I can bring them to you if you'd like," Phillip said.

"Phillip, I don't believe you're helping matters. Haven't I told you over the years, sometimes too much information is just too much? Can't you see she's upset? Pete, sweetheart, have a seat. I have a book that might help you. I've been keeping records of these happenings for thousands of years. And I have information that may help you. It's nearly noon, and I can see that everyone is tired. I'll leave this for you, and I'll come back at sunset. If you have any questions, perhaps we can answer them for you then." James had always been the most diplomatic of the group and was calming and assuring in ways no one else could manage.

~~~

That evening when Aaron arose, he found Pete in his study waiting for him. If he had been honest with himself, he was not really surprised. He had found her to be extremely determined when she set her mind on something. She also had the book that James had given her. The mark was different this time.

"It's finished, the mark, it's finished growing. I don't know how I know that, but I know."

She was glowing with beauty. Beautiful and something more, something he couldn't quite put his finger on, but if he had to guess he would say she looked fertile. But it was not so much for herself but for everything around her. All living things — a natural magick, he thought.

The vine had made its way to her face and one vivid green leaf was centered over her eye, covering about two inches up and below it. Another vine came across her neck and stopped just to the center of her throat. The leaves here were of varying shades of green and artistically arranged. There were buds and flowers here and there, but the overall effect was ethereal.

"You are incredibly beautiful, Piccadilly," Aaron told her.

"I've been looking at this book of Mr. James'. I want you to forbid Dominic and the others to help me with my family. It's too dangerous, and someone could get hurt." She was not going to comment on his observations, he noticed with a smile. And that, too, did not surprise him.

"I'm afraid I can't do that, and even if I could, I doubt very highly that anyone would listen to me, even as their master. Dominic would die for you; you are his mate. He has no choice but to protect you, as I have no choice when it comes to protecting Sara and the children," he told her calmly.

"You have to, don't you see? I've been taking notes. I wrote down all the traits that each of my brothers have, a list of their powers, and their physical characteristics that I could remember when I lived there. They aren't human. I have to concede that my mother is a nymph, but she isn't limited to what's in this book either. None of them are. They are as different as you and I."

Aaron looked at her. She did not understand yet. She did not understand what her relationship with Dominic, with all of them, was going to mean for her. His heart went out to her.

"Let's get you to breakfast before Sara eats it all, and then we'll talk. Where is Dominic this fine evening?" She plopped down hard in the chair opposite the desk where he sat. Her face flamed up at his question.

"He's...we...he and I, we... You know, I've never met anyone who is so obsessed with someone's sex life like you people are." She looked away from him.

"Ah. But I didn't mention sex, love, you did. Never mind, I get the idea. Wore him out, did you, just so you could speak to me alone? I may be a very old vampire, but I am in love too. You'd do anything to keep him safe, including fucking him to exhaustion so you could try and convince me to see things your way. Smart woman, but I doubt he'll appreciate it much, will you, Dominic?"

Pete jerked around to see Dominic standing in the doorjamb. Aaron thought Dominic looked mad, well, probably pissed. Really, really pissed would be a better description, he thought.

"You're right, I don't. I'm not happy at all. May I have a word or two with Piccadilly alone, sire?"

She turned to Aaron. Aaron was sure Pete was about to throw herself at his mercy and beg for him to save her, but Dominic scooped her up over his shoulder and carried her out of the room. Aaron burst out laughing.

Then he decided to go and find his lovely wife. Maybe she was nursing the children again. Aaron wanted to watch her in her maternal glory. Watching her birth the children was one thing he knew he'd never forget, but seeing her suckle the babies...it made everything around him seem so small and unimportant.

~~~

When Dominic was halfway down the stairs to his lair, he started ranting at her. By the time he reached the lair, he was in a full blown anger.

"What did you think you were doing? Did you honestly think I would stand back and let you fight them on your own? You leave my bed, our bed, so you could make arrangements behind my back, to have me stand back and to...Damn it, I'm so..."

Dominic had put her down on her feet and was striding back and forth in the massive room when he stopped to make a point. He could not for the life of him remember what it had been because he looked at her, really looked at her. His breath caught and his heart skipped several beats. She was beautiful. Lovelier than he had ever seen a woman look, and she was his.

Dominic walked slowly toward her so that he could take all of her in. The marks on her face made her seem surreal and dreamlike. Her pale skin was translucent and it glowed. Her short hair seemed to have sparks of light flitting off from it in small shoots of electrical arcs. Her body had always been tiny to him, but seemed more delicate and fragile somehow. When he reached her, he cupped her face in his hands and kissed her, gently at first, and then hunger took over. He could not seem to get enough of her.

"Baby, I love you. I want you to know that. More than anything on this earth, I love you. But I need you to let me help you. I need to protect you. You're mine, Piccadilly Fresno Marshall."

He kissed her again and again. He felt her hug him to her.

"I've never been in love before. I don't even know if I believe this is real. It's all happened so quickly."

"Believe it love. I am yours through all eternity," Dominic whispered through her mind.

"How did you do that?" Shock laced Pete's voice.

"We are bonded and mated, by blood and through sex. You and I have a special way of communicating that no one will ever hear or cut off. Even in death we will have a bond. I love you, Pete." He held her close, the need to hold and to be held by her overwhelming.

Dominic needed to protect her, and needed her to realize that he was going to do it no matter what she said. He loved her, loved her with all his body and heart.

Need. Need to protect her, to dominate her, was strong. He pressed his cock into her belly and her immediate response made him groan. Her arousal and her scent hit his senses like a hard hit to his groin. Through their bond, he showed her what he wanted, down on her knees, her mouth around his cock.

"Yes, baby, oh yes."

She did not wait for him to tell her again, but dropped to her knees in front of him. She slowly traced her hands up his massive thighs then reached up and unbuckled the belt at his pants, taking her time, never taking her eyes from his. After she pulled it free of the loops, she ran her hands down the front of him, cupping his cock hard between her hands. As much as he wanted to close his eyes to savor her touching him, he could not take his eyes from hers.

Pete took her time opening each button of his pants, pulling his briefs down with the pants, kissing his skin as she exposed it. When his cock sprang free, she licked the tip very softly, making Dominic hiss with need.

"You're killing me, Pete. Please have mercy on me. Take me into your wet mouth. Please."

He watched as she wrapped her hand around his cock at the base and slid it up slowly. His cock pulsed in her hand. When she reached the swollen head, she looked again into his eyes. She had his full attention now. Then she flicked out her tongue and licked the pearl of cum at the eye of his cock. Her eyes fluttered closed. Her moan nearly had him coming all over her face. He surged his cock forward and into her hot mouth. It seemed to glide down the back of her throat, engulfing him in her heat. He growled and tipped his head back. The sensations ricocheting through him, touching every nerve in his body, made him forget to be gentle. He pumped into her hard and fast. And then she pulled away. He looked down at her again, ready to beg her to take him back into her mouth, but she stopped him with a look.

She ran her mouth down the entire length of him, nipping and biting. He loved it when she alternated between hard and gentle bites. But he wanted to watch her take him into her mouth again. With his hand, he cupped her head and then guided her back to his cock, telling her without words what he wanted from her. Every time his cock slipped out of her mouth, slick and wet, and then disappeared again into the heat, it made him want to go faster, harder. He suddenly needed to be inside of her, needed to come inside of her feminine heat. He pulled from her mouth, still hard, still erect, and yanked her up against his body.

"Baby, Pete, I want to come inside of you. I want to fuck that tight pussy of yours from behind again."

She stood up and bent over the chair again, but he had other ideas and guided her to the bed. He had her get onto it and on all fours, spreading her legs wide for him. He came up behind her and smacked her ass. When she went to move away from him, he held her still with a hand on her back and growled hard and mean.

"You've been a bad girl, Piccadilly, going to my master and telling him to keep me away. What do you think you were going to prove? I'm gonna spank you. Spank this tight ass until its red. Then I'm going to fuck you, fuck you until you scream."

Dominic brought his hand down twice more across Pete's ass, watching it pink up with his prints. He switched hands and slapped her twice more. Her bottom was beautifully pink now. He reached between her legs and felt her juices dripping down her thighs. He inserted two of his fingers and touched her deep inside.

He wanted to taste her. Now. He wanted to lick her thighs clean and feel her come in his mouth. But his need to dominate her was stronger.

"Are you going to go behind my back again, Pete? Will you leave here without protection? Answer me, damn it. Now!" He brought his hand down hard on her ass again.

His cock ached, hurt from the need to be deep inside of her. If he did not feel her walls tighten around him soon, he felt as if he would explode.

Moving to her core, teasing her with his cock, he leaned over her, forcing her head to the mattress while her ass was still up. He could see her juices trickling down her thighs, curls wet with her own need. He reached under her and flicked her clit and was rewarded with a moan.

"Answer me, Pete. When you answer me, I'll fuck you. I'll ram my cock deep into you and make you come." His voice was low, need making it raspy.

"No, I won't, no. Please, I won't leave without...Dominic, now I need you now." She was begging him, begging and agreeing, just what he needed to hear.

He slammed into her deep and pulled back to surge forward hard and fast again and again. His release was close.

He leaned over her and whispered in her ear, "Come with me, baby. Come with me now." He nuzzled her shoulder and up to her neck and bit her, bringing them both to a hard release.

CHAPTER FIFTEEN

After they showered, together this time, they went to the upper floors. Aaron didn't mention that he had seen the couple already that night, and no one was the wiser. He knew what it was like. He and Sara still could not get enough of each other. A simple look or a touch could send them into need that would be embarrassing if it wasn't so deliciously fun.

"I'd like to say something, if you don't mind." Pete, the name everyone had agreed suited her much better than Piccadilly, looked at the people assembled in the room. "I've looked over this journal and I want to tell you that while I appreciate you wanting to help me, my family isn't your problem. No, wait, let me finish. I know that you think because Dominic and I have something, and I'm not sure what it is yet, but because we have this thing, that doesn't mean you have to risk your lives for me. These men are dangerous, more dangerous than what you have in this book. I won't have anyone getting hurt for me out of a sense of duty or obligation to a woman you just met."

"Are you quite through, young lady? I must say that I'm hurt and not a little disappointed. To think that I would not want to help you is just mean. I have grown quite fond of you. And I do not have many that I call friend. Do you think that I have hooked my pony to a stupid person? I do not; I consider you my friend. Now, I do not know about the rest of this household, and they had better think on it carefully because Miss Penny is with me on this. I'm standing beside you, in front of you or behind you. I don't really care, but I will be there, wherever you need me. Besides, I have taken a liking to that ridiculous name you call me and I do not believe I could stand to hear it if you were not around to say it to me."

That was the longest speech anyone had ever heard Duncan give. Pete walked over to the older gentleman and kissed him hard on the mouth. With tears in her eyes, she leaned in to his ear and told him how much she thought of him too. And also, it was horse, not pony.

"Well, if that silliness is over, then let us get down to business, shall we? You mentioned you looked through James' book; tell them what you have found, and I shall bring in some snacks for everyone."

No one said a word as Duncan wiped away the tears on his cheek. Aaron felt his own eyes water at Duncan's speech. Aaron decided that he needed to do something special for his friend, something the older man would enjoy.

"I've made a list of each of my brothers after I looked at what you had listed for each being described in here. You know, their eye color, hair, what they seem to be able to do, something like you've done here, see?"

Pete, with tears still in her eyes, handed around the stacks of paper she had printed out, giving each person a copy. Aaron was at first overwhelmed, then impressed with the way she had laid out and put everything together.

"I went through the book carefully and matched each trait to the being on the page. Some of them overlapped a little, but I noted that. In the first column is their name and birthdates; that seemed important to you, Mr. James. For them, I don't know how much help it will be, but I marked in anyway. The second is their physical descriptions, any markings that I might have seen, and tattoos they had when I was a child."

"I put the dates there to keep track of how long they lived. You can tell a great deal about a being that way. Where they've lived, whose lives they've touched. Why, I once—"

"James, do you think we can hold off on that until later? Her family will be arriving soon and I, for one, would like to know what we are up against."

"Of course, Aaron. I'm so excited, you see. This is so wonderful. Sad but wonderful. It's a shame that we'll need to kill them all. Continue, child."

Pete looked stunned for a minute. Whether from James' enthusiasm or his statement that they would need to kill her family wasn't clear. After Pete stared at James for a moment longer, she continued on where she had stopped.

"A lot could have happened in all this time. Someday, I'd like you to show me how you can tell the difference between a mark, sigil, and a tattoo, please. The third and fourth columns are how they obtained the power and what it is or does. When I knew for sure that it was Sherman, I put the 'S' next to the power. That will be helpful to a point, but it's been almost nine years, so a lot could have happened between then and now. He could have taught them how to raise the dead by now for all I know. The last column is who my mother claims their father is or was. That should be taken with a grain of salt. She told me that I was the child of a king for a few months. Of course, she might have been talking about someone else, but...well, there you have it. That may or may not be accurate. She was consistent with what she told us, but I image a good liar would be able to keep it straight, don't you think?"

Aaron watched a very confident woman as she went over the documentation she had given them, then when she sat down, he saw a very shy little girl take her place.

"This is very well done. I must say, I'm impressed. You did all of this in one day? Good heavens, think what you could do with more time. Yes, it will be my upmost pleasure to show you anything you'd like to know about anything I know, but the tradeoff will be to teach me how to do this. Oh yes, I'm quite impressed."

James was beside himself. He had not had anyone take his book or his musings this seriously in a very, very long time and Aaron was happy to see Pete had brought a smile to his face.

"We have to discuss Sherman's part in all this. Mel said she would like to have a private chat with Pete and Dominic first, and then she would share what she knows with everyone else. She is understandably upset. And no matter how much I've tried to tell her this is not her fault, she feels that she should have done more to keep everyone safe." Aaron pulled Sara into his arms. She was taking this just as hard as Mel, and felt just as responsible.

"When do you think they'll arrive, Aaron? Soon? And what kind of plan do you have in the works to take care of this?" Colin was a warrior of old and details were important to him. Aaron, a warrior himself, understood this in him and appreciated it.

"They will be here within the next forty-eight hours, maybe a little longer if I can make it happen. They're moving slowly. They seem to keep having car trouble." Aaron grinned at that. His helpers were having a good time slowing down Pete's family, maybe a little too much fun. He wished he could join them, but he was needed here.

"I believe that we need to stay together, form a united front now and when they get here. Aaron, do you have any objections to us using this house as a base?" Dominic asked him.

"No," Pete said quickly. "I'm sorry, but the babies are here. I...we can't risk them. Somewhere else, please?"

"You are quite right," Aaron agreed with her. "We will take the babies away from the house. I think they would love a visit with their Uncle Demetrius and Aunt April in Molavonta Keep. What do you think, Sara?"

Mel was the Mistress of Light, and Sara's cousin. Mel actually lived in a very large castle in another realm different than the human world. They would be safe there, very safe, as the castle also had its own royal guard. Aaron liked this idea very much.

"I think that's a wonderful idea." Sara agreed readily with a glare at her mate. "They would be well tended and cared for, yes. Thank you for the suggestion, Pete."

Aaron knew better than to say that he had hoped Sara would stay with the children in the Keep as well, but he knew that it would be safer if he did not mention it to her.

"I knew you were a very smart man the first time I saw you. And you are right. I would have hurt you very badly. I think I might have a sexy little number that I bought with you in mind. I'll model it for you when my body is mine again. I love you, Aaron." Sara had heard his thoughts, apparently, and whispered through his mind her approval.

"You did not think I was a smart man when you met me. You told me you didn't care if that rogue killed me or not, just before you sliced off his head. And I love you too. Now pay attention, I want to get this meeting finished so I can ravish my mate later."

Nearly three hours later, they had a plan. Pete was never to be alone, this was a given, of course. The women seemed to feed off of each other's powers, strength in numbers it seemed, so it was logical that they would work together. Also, they were all going to help Pete meet her full potential by training her how to use and control her powers.

Pete had finally given up trying to tell them that she did not want the one curse she had, and certainly did not want to add to her misery. She spent the rest of the evening and nearly the new day doing things she did not know she could. And actually having fun.

"Sire, if I could have a word with you, please? In private."

Dominic had been dreading this conversation all evening. He was still getting used to Aaron as his master. The man who he had been a subject to before had been a horrific man, flaying vampires while still alive or staking them in the sun long enough for them to burn for the most minor of infractions. He was not sure how he was going to react to his news.

Aaron said that was fine, and asked if the study would be all right. The two of them walked to the room as if it were a guillotine and one or both of them was about to die.

"Come, man, out with it; the anticipation is killing me." They had been in the room five minutes with neither of them speaking. Dominic was having one argument with himself right after the other. He began unbuttoning his shirt and watching for a reaction from his master as he spoke.

"I've mated with Pete, sire, as you know, and—"

"Hold," Aaron said, exasperation in his voice. "My name is Aaron. Not 'sire,' not 'master,' and not even 'Mr.

MacManus.' I think I would prefer most anything to being called 'sire.' I'm your master, yes. But Dominic, I'm also your friend."

Dominic lost his train of thought. He'd always referred to Aaron by his first name, but had never called him that to his face. He wasn't sure if he could do so now, but was willing to try.

"Thank you, Aaron. I'll try and remember. It's about Pete and I. We've mated and bonded; we've exchanged blood. This isn't her fault. I bit her first, you see. I knew the story about Colin and Shade, but I still bit her. I love her. Please don't punish her. I take full responsibility for this." He bared his left shoulder, and there, wrapped around his bicep, was vine, and exact match to Pete's without the flowers.

"It started growing on me last night, I guess. I could feel it, but I didn't know what it was. It was just itchy at first. I beg of you, master, don't blame Pete. She had nothing to do with this."

The silence was profound. Dominic started to fidget, and stopped. When the answer came, it was not at all what he had expected. Nothing even close to it.

"You expect me to do what to her, Dominic? Kill her? Maim her in some hideous way? I thought that we had move beyond that, you and I. I'm disappointed. Not in you, but in myself. I should have tried harder to make you feel safe and secure here, but I've failed you. I'm sorry. You and your mate did nothing wrong, Dominic. Nothing, do you hear me? You love her and she you. This was fated, not planned. She is as welcome in this Kiss as any of you. Sara is excited about having another woman around. She seems to think that the two of them are already good friends. You won't let me disappoint my mate by moving away, will you?"

Dominic kneeled before the man. He was wrong not to have trusted Aaron. He had lived for so long with tyranny that he almost missed something very important standing right in front of him. A true friend.

"No, sire…Aaron. No, we aren't planning to move away. I know that I have pledged myself to you before, but I do so now with my heart, not my head. Before I wanted freedom, now, sire, if you would but give me a chance, I pledge to you with my heart and I ask you for your friendship. I meant no disrespect to you. I would—"

"Enough, Dominic! Christ. You are my friend. I welcome you into my heart, as well as my Kiss. And if you call me sire once more, I'm going to be a very unhappy vamp. Now, go be with your mate. You might need to know some of the things Pete is learning too." The two men embraced and moved back into the living room where things were just starting to get interesting.

CHAPTER SIXTEEN

"Pete, honey, please put my father back down on the floor. He's rather old and maybe fragile." Pete grinned at Mel. She loved upsetting Queenie. It was almost worth the stupid curse for that alone. And, not that she would tell these guys, she was having a blast learning how to control the thing.

"Melody Keeper, I'll have you know that I am not fragile and I would really appreciate it if one or all of you would please stop teaching her this particular trick. I no longer find it to be amusing to be lifted up in the air. Now, please put me down, dear. You have done it perfect eight times already and I don't like being the guinea hog."

Pete gently lowered Phillip to the floor, thinking that she should have maybe held him there just a little longer for pulling a knife at her back. Of course, if he had not have, they would not know all they knew about her now.

"Its pig, not hog, sir. Miss Pete, err Pete taught me that one quite some time ago."

Duncan had just entered the room with a large platter of food. Keeping the ladies of this family fed was a full time job evidently, and he and Penny seemed to love every minute of it. And they loved finding recipes off the Internet and trying make them together. Pete was glad that she had showed him out to search for them.

Daniel had joined the party sometime while Aaron and Dominic had been gone. He told her he had wanted to talk to her about the security set up she had had him put in. Just a few questions. But he seemed to be enjoying the lessons going on more. He turned to Duncan as he set down a large platter of what looked like giant hoagies.

"How's it hangin' there, Dunc, my man?" Daniel always asked the man this same question every time they were saw each other.

"Oh yes, I know this one. 'Low and to the left, low and to the left.' I was told to repeat it when I said it. Did I do it correctly, Miss Pete?" Duncan looked around the room that had suddenly gotten very quiet. "Did I not say it the right way?"

"Hummm, Dunc, has Eon been hanging around you in the kitchen lately?" Pete felt she knew the answer, but wanted to be sure.

"Why, yes, he has. A very nice young man, Master Eon. But I do believe he is not what he seems. We will need to investigate that more soon, I believe. Master Daniel, please have a few sandwiches. We have plenty."

Duncan delivered his line and his food and exited stage left as it were. Pete burst out laughing at the stunned look on Daniel's face.

Poor Dunc. Who would explain to him what that statement meant? Pete decided to have a little talk with Eon next time she saw him. Goodness, what if little Brent said something like that to Shade or Colin? She looked at the couple from across the room and thought they looked as if they could handle it.

The meeting with Mel happened just after they finished with the first set of the lessons. Pete and Dominic had met in of all places, a palace. Molavonta Castle Keep, the castle of the queen. The room they were lead to she'd been told was the queen's personal chambers and few had ever been inside.

"I wanted to tell you personally about the man in your past. Sherman, the man from your home, is...was my mate. He tried to have me step down by causing me to have a miscarriage. He is more evil than you can ever imagine."

Pete didn't say anything, but looked at Dominic. Something wasn't adding up. This was not the Queenie that Pete had come to dislike.

"He was also instrumental in the kidnapping of Shade and Brent a few months ago. Sherman planned to kill them both. Brent was a pawn. He...Brent was unharmed by Sherman, but he could have been...Sherman could have killed him too."

"So, this is your fault? You're to blame for my family being as powerful as they are? Gee, Queenie, you really are an awful person, aren't you? I mean, to know that he was doing all this and being aware of it. Well, that makes you more evil, doesn't it?"

Pete felt Dominic trying to get her to stop, to not say those things, but Pete knew this was an important step for them both. She and the queen had had their differences, but this was personal. This was something that went beyond their boundaries as women of magic.

"Of course I didn't know what he was doing! Do you think I would have allowed him to continue if I had of known? Do you think if I had known he had taken that little boy, I would have let him? Do you think that I would not have put a stop to whatever involvement he has in your family's evil? I wouldn't have stopped it immediately."

Magic shimmered in the air, hot and heavy. Dominic did not move. Pete stood up, walked over to the queen, and hugged her. "Yeah, I know you would have. But you didn't know, so stop beating yourself up over it. What's done is done. Now...now, Queenie, we kill the bastard."

~~~

Pete had a business to run and after the meeting with Mel that had lasted until early morning, she sat down in the kitchen with the house phone and took care of a few things. She made two calls to suppliers and another to Toby, setting up a time to have the wiring and other equipment delivered to Colin's house.

Colin had asked her last night if she could come by and set up their computer equipment and the game system. He had been impressed when he'd seen what Aaron's system could do and wanted to get started. She told him she would do what she could, as she was limited on her movements while her family was coming for her. Then she called Mr. Mackey.

"Hello, this is Pete Bartholomew; I'd like to leave a message for Mr. Mackey or Ms. Mackey to call me back at this number, please."

The person who had answered was not Shelia this time, and Pete wondered what had happened to her. She thought she was a great person. Pete knew she was Mackey's daughter and loved the fact that he'd made her work for a living.

"Yes, Ms. Bartholomew, could you hold, please? I'll only be a moment."

"Ah, sure, but I just wanted to leave a message—" She realized that as soon as she said "sure" she had been put on hold.

154

Duncan set a large platter of food in front of her. She looked up at him then back down at the food. She was going to weigh as much as this house if they kept this up.

"You do know that I don't eat this much food in a week, right? I do know when I'm hungry. And come to think of it, why are you always feeding me?"

The voice from the ear piece of the phone at Pete's ear answered for Duncan. "If I know anything about women, it's that they don't eat near enough most of the time. Good morning, Ms. Bartholomew. I'm glad you called."

Mr. Mackey himself was on the phone.

"Mr. Mackey, I didn't mean for her to get you. I was more than willing to leave a message for you to call at your next opportunity." She found herself straightening up in her chair as if he could see her. She slumped back down with a frown.

"As it so happens, this is perfect timing on your part. When can you come in to see me? The sooner the better, actually. I just need a couple of hours to set up with Shelia, if that's okay."

Meeting for what? she wondered, and looked over at Duncan. "Hang on a sec, let me check with someone. I have to clear a few things with the people I'm staying with." She turned to Duncan and stared at him, hoping he could help her out. He reached out, took the phone from her, and pushed the hold button on the hand set.

"You look a little shell-shocked, Ms. Pete. What has happened? Shall I call Master Bradley? That man on the phone, he did not threaten you, did he? Why I'll have you know I was quite the boxer in my day." Duncan danced around the room with his fists up and bounced on his toes like a professional. Then he smiled at her.

"No," Pete said with a small laugh. "It's Mr. Mackey. He wants me to come in to see him. I do need to talk to him, but I promised Dominic that I wouldn't leave the house without him. Dunc, I have a business to run. It's not much, but there are people that depend on me to help them. I can't walk away from a call because I might or might not run into trouble. I don't want to make Dominic mad either."

Although, if she thought about Dominic when he was mad at her the last time, she thought it just might be worth making him upset again. The last time had been so...so delicious. She squirmed in her seat. Just thinking about it got her all hot and bothered.

"Why not take the ladies of the house with you, Miss Pete? Her ladyship and Lady Shade would love to go out, I'm sure. I believe you would be quite safe with the two of them in tow. The day nanny is here for the children and Miss Penny and I are on hand as well. There is also the matter of your clothing. Was it not pointed out that you might be running low on certain items?"

She and Dunc both colored a little at that, and yes, he was right. Dominic was a little rough on her underwear and wow, another jolt to her groin area. She pushed the hold button again before her train of thought went too far off course.

"Mr. Mackey, I was wondering if we could meet, say, at two this afternoon? I have other business I need to attend to beforehand, and if that's okay with you, I could meet you around then. But I don't...hummm...as you remember, I don't do dress up. Is that still okay?" She barely owned jeans and t-shirts much lest business attire.

"Yes, that's fine, fine indeed. You wear what's most comfortable to you. I've been wearing ties for so long...well, it's my new comfortable I think," Mackey told her with a chuckle. "Two will be fine with me. I look forward to seeing you again, Pete."

Pete was nervous now. She needed to find Sara and Shade and then convince them to spend time with her on a shopping spree. Like Pete had any idea how to go shopping at all much less on a "spree." Pete found Sara in the nursery.

Pete did not step into the room, but watched as Sara nursed the little boy. Pete had not seen the babies since she had delivered them. She didn't have a lot of experience with kids. Spending one afternoon with Brent was okay, but the babies were so tiny yet.

"You should come in and meet them. They aren't so small anymore," Sara told her without looking up from her son.

"I don't want to intrude. I'll talk to you later." She started to walk away when Sara called her back.

"No, this is perfect, Pete. Come in and meet your namesake. Well, sort of namesake. I'm so glad I didn't know about your real first name when we named Mac after you. Can you image how much trouble a name like Aaron Piccadilly MacManus would give him? But he'll be just like his father and slay the infidel, I'm afraid. Anyway, his name is Pete, Aaron Pete, but we'll call him Mac." Mac stared at Pete as if he knew who she was, and what she had done for him. "Why don't you hold him?"

"Oh no, I don't know how. He's little, isn't he? No, I'll just talk to him this way. His bruise looks good, doesn't it?" And it did, it really did, Pete thought.

"Nonsense! Sit down. Here, hold Lizzy. Her real name is Melody Savannah Elizabeth MacManus, but we'll call her Lizzy." Sara just simply handed her the tiny bundle of pink.

The babies had their own beds in the big nursery. Plus everything one could ever want for a new baby, and as soon as they were old enough, they would have their own rooms as well.

This room was perfect as a room for babies. The walls were a light wainscoting that was nearly halfway up the cream-colored walls. The hardwood floors, also a light oak, had throw rugs scattered all over. The pink side of the room had bright pink curtains and pink bed set. Dolls of every imaginable size, shape and color were loaded onto several shelves. There were even pink books on the lower shelf. The blue side of the room was blue everywhere the opposite was pink, including the blue books. But instead of dolls, there were balls, bats and mitts. She could even see that there were several trucks and cars lined up in neat rows.

"You think this one is going to have any less trouble with her name?" Pete looked at the little girl in her arms and fell in love.

Lizzy was a beauty even at one week. Her hair was as red as her mother's, long and thick too. Her skin was so soft it defied words. Her eyes were the deepest blue that Pete had ever seen, and she looked so serious. Pete would swear there was a tiny frown between her eyes, just like her father's. But she had her mother's coloring and her lips.

Pete tried one of the tricks she had been taught last night and opened her mind to the baby. She immediately felt the connection. And unbelievably, Lizzy spoke to her. Not in words, but in images and sounds.

"Shit! Sorry, she...she spoke to me. I don't know why that should surprise me. She's called to me before. But this time, she actually spoke to me. Told me she liked me, and that I'm pretty." She felt the goofy grin, but couldn't seem to stop it from spreading.

"She called to you? When?"

Pete looked up at Sara at the sudden tone in her voice.

"When her brother was in trouble the day they were born. That's why I showed up at the restaurant. She sent out this, I don't know, an alarm, I guess. I just followed it and there you were. No big deal." And it hadn't been either, not really.

"You have unborn children talk to you all the time, do you?"

Pete could tell Sara had meant it as a joke, but as Pete did indeed talk to all sorts of people, she answered her seriously. Turning back to the baby, she told her the truth. "No. Not all the time. And not always kids. Sometimes there are adults that are in comas who will call out. I used to drive myself nuts trying to do what they wanted, but I couldn't keep up. Some of the things they wanted were like last requests, you know? No one believed me, of course. So to offer comfort, I'd tell them that it had been done or I had told whatever it was they wanted said to their family. I know that's lying to them, but trying to get people to believe that this family member who has been out of it for like ten years suddenly wants them to forgive and forget is hanky."

"I would guess it would. How long did you do this before you figured out that you could tone them down? I would guess it had been years."

"I could hear them as a kid, just little voices in my head. Then as I hit puberty, they got louder all the time. You believed me, though. I guess it was because of your own magic. Anyway, that's another reason I clamp down so hard. It's like a super highway of requests. It used to give me major headaches." Pete did not look up. She was afraid of what she might see on Sara's face.

"Yes, I can see where that would be an issue. Pete, have you told anyone else about this? Shared this even with Dominic?" Sara asked her quietly.

Pete watched Sara stand and bring the now sleeping Mac over and gently lay him in her arms. Lizzy had fallen asleep while Pete had been talking to her mom, but Sara took her anyway.

"No. I didn't think to tell Dominic. And before that…no, I thought it was better that people didn't think I was more nuts than they already did. I'm not even sure why I told you, to be honest. I'm not normally a share all kind of girl."

Sara laughed and sat back down with Lizzy. Pete kept staring at the baby in her arms and wondered what it would be like to have one of her own. A baby of Dominic's. She wasn't sure he even wanted kids and decided that the next time they were together and not trying to jump each other's bones, she'd ask him. It would probably be about fifty years from now.

"I really came up here to ask for your help. Well, not really help, but Dominic doesn't want me to leave the house without him…actually, without protection, he said. I have an appointment at two that I need to go to. I have this job thingy, and I need the money for stuff. Dunc…I mean, I was wondering if you and Mrs. Larimore would go with me? I have some things I have to get at Wally World too, you know underwear and stuff. You don't have to go into the appointment with me or anything; I think I can handle that. Then I have to go over to the Larimore mansion to do some light install work, nothing major. What do you think?"

Pete looked down at Mac. He was a real doll baby. He had the deep blue eyes his sister had, but his hair was curly and dark. His nose was his mom's, but he was his father's image in every other way, including the serious expression he was giving Pete.

Sara did not ask Pete why she needed the money and she was glad for that. And no matter how mad Dominic got, Pete knew she would go on this run, with or without the two women. She had had a life before Dominic and he was just going to have to get used to her doing what she needed to get things done.

Pete frowned slightly, wondering about him. He had told her last night that he was almost seven hundred years old. And that he had been turned when he was in his late twenties. Did he have a family? She knew they would not be alive, she was not stupid, but would he have any long lost relatives? And what if once he met her family, he didn't want her anymore except to eat? She refused to call it "feed."

Her breath caught when she felt him move through her. Dominic was still asleep, but his warmth and love suddenly surrounded her. Life was suddenly just peachy, she thought with a huge grin.

Chapter Seventeen

The three of them showed up at the Mackey building at one-thirty. Pete was glad that they had stopped shopping finally. She didn't think that buying underwear was going to be such an event that would require three hours. And the women would not let her shop at her usual store either. Wal-Mart had been fine when she didn't have a mate, they had told her, but now she needed to buy with Dominic in mind. Pete could not make them understand he didn't care what she had on; he would just rip it out of his way anyway. They laughed at her for nearly three hours about that, teasing her mercilessly.

So Pete bought eight dollar panties and a fifty dollar bra at a boutique, not a store. She had to admit, even if only to herself, that they did feel really sexy against her skin. The silk sliding across her felt so much different than the cotton briefs she normally wore. She didn't tell them that when they said that she needed to buy for Dominic, she thought they meant he wore women's panties, but knowing these two, they probably knew that anyway.

"Hello, Ms. Bartholomew. I'll let Mr. Mackey know that you're here. If you ladies wouldn't mind having a seat, I'll be right with you."

The new receptionist showed them to a really pretty room. She had then offered them drinks and had handed Pete a remote to the large screened television before leaving them in the private waiting room.

"You work for the Mackey Corporation? Gee, they're a big deal in the were world. Aaron said they own twenty-five businesses that only employ were," Shade told her in awe.

Pete looked around the room. This was nice, she supposed, but then she didn't know what constituted as a "big deal" in any world.

"I don't know anything about this company other than what I do with their computers and software issues. I just did some freelance stuff for him. He's one of my part-timers. I want to see if he'll help me out on another project."

She wanted to see if he could maybe take on a couple of college students per quarter for them to gain experience before graduating. It would help them out once out in the business world, give Mr. Mackey some cheap labor, and it looked good on the student's resume too. It worked out well for everyone really. At least she hoped it would.

Someone came in the door just as she was about to explain the project to the two of them. Sara introduced him as Bradley Wolff, the alpha. He and Sara had known each other for a while and Shade had worked with him concerning Brent at one time, as well. If Bradley was surprised that all three of them were there, he did not let on. He shook her hand and told her that Karl Mackey had called him just after she had left the other day and told him about all she had done for his company.

"I can see Karl was right about the beauty part. I'm willing to believe he is correct about your computer skills as well. He also said that you were smart, articulate, and had a take no prisoners attitude that he envied. He had thought himself a hard ass until he met you. He was really impressed with your attitude about performances and if it wasn't up to standard and beyond, then they were history. I agree with you, it's the only sure way to make a business work."

Pete turned away from him shyly. She knew that he could see her new mark, everyone could. It had actually caused a little commotion at the boutique earlier. But Shade had helped Pete through it by changing the direction of the shop owner's attention toward a dress or something. Pete had been so grateful to her, and still was actually. Everyone thought it was a tattoo. Only other supernaturals like Bradley would be able to tell it wasn't a tat. But the part about the business, she didn't know anything about that; she just went with her gut. Making money and getting ahead was all anyone wanted out of life really.

When the receptionist told them that everyone was waiting, and turned to lead them to a very large conference room, Pete felt her heart rate start to rise. She stiffened, and stopped just outside the door. The room was full of people, so many in fact that some were leaning against the walls as well as sitting in all the chairs.

"I had an appointment with Mr. Mackey. I'm sorry but there's been a mistake. I don't know what's going on." Pete hated the panic in her voice, but she couldn't help it. Crowds of people made her nervous. Especially now, she was even less sure of herself. Suddenly, she felt Dominic sweep into her.

"Love, are you all right? I can feel you're scared. Come back to bed, let me hold you," he whispered to her.

"I'm not there. I mean, I'm outside of the house. I'm with Sara and Shade. We went shopping and I had a meeting. There's this appointment that I had, but it's all wrong. I don't like people and there are so many..."

He did not say anything for several seconds, but she could feel his anger just like it was her own. He was trying to control it, but he was very upset with her and afraid for her too.

"I thought we agreed that you'd wait for me to leave the house. Pete, you must learn to obey me. I need to keep you safe. You're mine, and I keep what is mine."

His anger and disappointment roared through her. Where he had made her feel good earlier, he now made her angry and hurt. And it made her own temper rise. "Obey you? I don't need a father at this stage of my life, buster, but thanks all the same. Listen here, you arrogant ass, I've been taking care of myself for a lot longer than you have. And so far, I've done a pretty good job. I will come and go as I please, when I please, and where the fuck I please. If you don't like that, then you can just fuck the hell off."

Pete was pissed off and wanted to cause bodily harm to a man three times her size. How smart was that? But she did do something very mean and sent him an image of her in her new panties and bra set she had bought, then took a mental eraser and rubbed out her body, leaving just her head there. Then she stuck her tongue out at him. She hoped he got the message because she shut the door to him mentally, not waiting for his reply.

Stupid ass-wipe! He would rue the day he tried to make her try to stay like a lap dog. Next thing you know, she thought, he'll have me barefoot, pregnant and in the kitchen. "I don't do the little woman routine," she muttered aloud. She looked up at Shade who had a strange smile on her face.

"You okay now? They can be such cavemen when they want to be, can't they? Oh no, I didn't listen in, not that I could when it's a mate thing, but I could tell by the expression on your face. Plus, I think you should know that when you are highly emotional as you are now, your eyes glow and your hair sparks. It's really an amazing sight."

"Shit! I forgot my glasses. No wonder that lady at the store...boutique looked at me funny when she gave me the price. I must have scared the crap right outta her." Pete giggled. The woman had been a bitch, and maybe she was glad just a little that she had forgotten them.

"Thanks, Mrs. Larimore, that helped."

"If you call me that once more, I'm gonna punch you in the nose. My name is Shade. Please call me that. That's what friends do, and I do think of you as my friend." Shade hugged Pete to her and they proceeded to the meeting. Being mad at Dominic and Shade calling her friend, for a reason she could not fathom, gave her newfound courage and confidence. She raised her chin high and stepped into the room.

Sitting around a large table were eighteen men and women, all of them were. At the head of the table was Bradley. He was their alpha, which made him their king wolf. He was the one who had asked Karl to set up this meeting, and Pete calling when she did only expedited it.

"I've called this meeting to introduce Ms. Pete Bartholomew to each of you, as she will hopefully be working with you all in the near future. I haven't had a chance to talk with Ms. Bartholomew yet, but hopefully, this will meet with her approval."

Bradley went around the table and told her who each person was, the company they were there representing, and a couple of issues he or she was having right now.

"All of you have read the report that Karl has had made for us, and as you can see, Ms. Barth...may I call you Pete?" He turned to her so fast she nearly jumped out of her chair.

"Ah, yeah, but it's Piccadilly. Just Pete is fine." She stammered a little, but felt good that she could make a full sentence.

"Good. Pete saved the Mackey Corporation ten million dollars over the next five years. Plus, she was able to save the company an untold amount of money by letting him know that an employee was using company funding to finance his gambling habit. Pete found a mistake in Karl's accounting software and security hardware. Recently, she took on Becca's Place as a client and the computer systems for that as well as Master MacManus' and Master Larimore's home and business securities respectively. Now, there isn't a company in here that can't benefit from that kind of help. I'd like to propose that we all hire Pete as our in house consultant. I'd like to have her set up an office in each of your offices and hire her own staffing to be there full time when she is off site. She would be in charge of any programming we have running, including security and finance. I'm sure there are a great deal more applications she could help us with as well." Bradley turned to Pete. "Well, Pete, will you come and play with us?" She stared at him with open mouth. Why the cheeky bastard!

"I can't work for you. What I mean is, I don't think I can work for you. Shit! Sorry. Let me start over." She drew a deep breath and looked at Shade and Sara, who had been invited to the meeting to make her feel more comfortable, Bradley had said, but also because of their prior involvement with the pack and himself.

"Please take your time. This is a lot to throw at you at one time. I had hoped to sit down with you and work out the details before this type of full scale meeting, but we also didn't want to wait and let someone else make you a job offer. I've no doubt we could compete if it came to that, but I want the best for this pack and from all accounts, you're it," he said in way of an apology.

"I think you might be overestimating my value a bit. Plus, Mr. Mackey only had me work for a few days and I found that stuff fairly easy. I mean, I could help you out, you know, consult or whatever, but work for you full-time? What am I supposed to do with all of the extra time after I get you all cleaned up and secure? You going to fire me? I need a steady income, Mr. Alpha. I have people who depend on me for financial help that I can't let down. This is a good offer, but like I said, I can't think that it'll work for either of us in the long run."

Her belly fluttered a little. These people could eat her for lunch if she pissed them off, she just realized. Literally.

"Pete, these men aren't the only group we have in our pack. These are just a few of the ones who could get away today. We also have several smaller and larger companies that are overseas. Believe me; we will be able to keep you busy for a very long time. Daniel Scott, I believe you've already worked with him, said that you suggested putting everyone on a large in-house server to make communications better. That alone he said would take you months to set up, and more to install and monitor.

"As for your financial help, I'm well aware of what you do with your income, and that would be a part of your hiring package. You would get a percentage of each savings you make the companies. Your salary will be paid weekly whether you work or not, but I don't foresee that happening much. I know that you work with the local colleges, taking kids out on jobs to help you so that they can get on-job experience; we want you to keep that up, it's good for the company image and a great deal of help to the communities. We believe in the same venue, give and it will give back to you. As for your donations, we have found out that you took a large portion of your payment from this company to fund a pet project of ours as well as yours. Becca's Place is something everyone in this room has a vested interest in. For every dollar you donate and each hour you work, or have your crew work at the house, the Brotherhood will donate equal time and money."

"Fuck. Sorry. How did you find...the teller? Should have known, it seems no one is what they seem, are they? I can't make this decision without thinking about it. I know it's a great deal, hell of a deal, but I won't make a decision without giving it at least one or two days of serious thought. I mean, I don't even own anything but jeans and tees. Not really a business suit person, then there's the traveling. I don't own a car, just a bike, not so nice in the winter months. Plus, Toby, I help him out sometimes. He's a very good friend and without his help, well, I don't know where I'd be right now. Not sitting here with you all, that's for sure. Did I mention I don't do people well? Well, I don't. My language is in the crapper, and I guess you figured that out too."

She was babbling again. She really hated when she did that, but could not seem to stop doing it when she was nervous.

"You'll be able to wear what you want, unless it's a formal meeting, and then only if it is required. As for travel, we have our own planes that would be at your disposal. There are even a few houses that are empty that you can take as a permanent residence on the pack grounds. A car will be provided for you, as well as a driver. Your language is crappy, but as long as you try to clean it up a bit, we should be okay. Pete..." Bradley leaned forward. "We really want this to work out for all of us. And you're right, you do need to think about this, and if I'm not mistaken, you have a mate of your own. He might want to be made aware of it as well. You take all the time you need and just call Karl here at his office if you have any questions. Plus, here's my private number and cell number. You think of anything, you just call one of us."

"Yeah, okay, I'll do that. But the mate part might be a moot point if I have to stake him later tonight." She looked up in alarm. She did not know if these people, these wolves, knew about Aaron and his Kiss. But Bradley simply threw back his head and laughed. She flushed a deep, hot red. Damn it, she really needed to start thinking before she spoke.

"Yes, we are aware of each other. And good luck with your mate. I'm sure he's as sorry as they come. Until then, Pete, I'd like to have a word or two with you about Eon in private, please." He'd asked politely, but she could hear the tension in his voice.

"Oh God, what's he done now? I swear whatever it is, I can fix it, but if it's something he's said, well, maybe I can just cut his tongue out. He's really a good kid. He just doesn't think before he speaks. Of course, I guess I do the same thing sometimes, but...well, that doesn't make it right, but it could be my fault. Probably is, so whatever he's done, I'll...I take full responsibility, all right? You just have to let me make sure he finishes his education. I know he doesn't act like it, but..."

Bradley was laughing at her. She might have noticed it sooner, because if the tears streaming down his face where any indication, he had been laughing for some time. But they had been walking down the hall to a nice office and it was not until she sat down across from him that she realized it.

"Think you could let me in on the joke maybe?"

He didn't answer right away because Daniel Taggert walked in and shook hands with Bradley. This was bad, she just knew it. Whatever Eon had done, it was bad.

"First, I want to tell you what I am. I know you are aware that I'm a shifter and a were, a werewolf actually. But I'm the alpha, the leader of this pack. All the men you met today, Daniel here included, answer to me and only me. Daniel has a unique situation in that he works for Aaron and does answer to him in business matters, but to me for pack issues. Nothing, and I mean nothing, goes on within my territory that I'm not made aware of. That being said, Daniel came to me the other day about Eon. I'll let him explain." Bradley leaned back in the big office chair and nodded to Daniel.

Pete just knew she was not going to like this, but Eon was her friend and she would stand up for him no matter what. If he really had done something so dreadful that they felt she needed to be told in private, well, she would be there for him and fuck these people.

"Pete, how much do you know about his background, Eon's I mean? Do you know his parents maybe or—"

"Look, I've always been a straight to the point sort of person. You know, rip the fuck...flipping Band-Aid right off and get on with it. If his mom is back again and trying to say he's done something wrong, well, he hasn't. I know him as well as anyone. I keep an eye on him. If she's asking for money, he doesn't have any of that either, at least as far as she's concerned. If she just wants him back, well fuck her, she can't have him. I have custody of him until he's eighteen and that's another five months. He's mine. So whatever it is, tell me."

"You have custody of him? You can't be much older than him, for Christ's sake!" Bradley exploded at her.

"Well, the courts didn't see a problem with it. He just needed to get away from that bitch and they knew it. I just have to make...what the fuck? I don't have to explain my actions to you or anyone else. Tell me what it's going to cost to fix and I'll work something out." Pete stood up and grabbed her bag that she had put on the stand next to the door when they walked in. She noticed that Daniel was looking at his boss, the King Ding-dong or whatever. She did not care if they could talk that mind thingy or not. As soon as they were done here, she was going back to Dominic and snuggling.

"Pete, I don't think we've handled this very well. Eon hasn't done anything wrong. He's a were, or at least part were. And as for his mother, well, I thank you for rescuing him from her if what you're saying is true about her, and I've no doubt that it is. He's a late bloomer, probably because he isn't a full blood." Bradley went onto explain. "Daniel came to me about him last week and asked my advice. I told him that he needed to discuss this with you before he talked to Eon. I take it that he's right, and Eon doesn't know."

"No, I don't think so. I don't think he's...hummm changed into anything either. I think I'd notice if he got fuzzy and howled at the moon once a month. Are you sure? I mean, could it be that he, fuck, I don't know, hangs with, like, dogs or something?" She was grasping at whatever she could. Eon was a werewolf. A friggin' werewolf?

"No, I'm sure. He has a scent about him. I'm surprised you haven't noticed it being that you're a supe too."

Daniel grinned at her. This was too much. Pete lowered her head into her hands and rested her elbows on her knees.

"Okay, it's been a weird few days, Mr. Alpha. I'm a wood nymph who is or isn't mated to a vampire. My friend is the cousin of the Queen of Magic and my work buddy is a werewolf. My brothers wanted to have a kid with me and let me see, did I forget anything? Oh yeah, I may or may not work for a pack of werewolves." She looked up at Bradley from between her fingers. "I think I need a drink."

Bradley winked at her and stood. "You're doing just fine. Better than most would, I think. I'm sorry, Pete. I wanted you to know before anything happens. If it's okay with you, I'll talk with Eon myself. As for the rest, trust me, you have good friends who'll see you through. And I'd really like it if you'd think of me as one of those friends." He walked with her to the door.

"What about Aaron? Who'll tell him? Oh, I guess he knows, huh? Good, it must have burned his butt not to have control over something first." She laughed when he did.

"I don't suppose you have any unattached sisters just like you around, do you? If you do, I'd really like to meet them if you don't mind."

They had met up with Sara and Shade who were watching some shopping channel with Shelia in her office.

"Nah, just maniacal brothers. But you're welcome to chew on them if you'd like." After it was out of her mouth, she realized what she had said and how it could be taken. Sheesh, she thought, she really needed to leave.

Bradley laughed again and assured her if she needed any help with them, just to let him know. He said that Aaron had told him what was happening with her family and he would be honored to be around to assist. She assumed at first he had meant at the house, but she was not so sure about anything anymore. She had become an honorary pack member when she saved the company money and made the donation to Becca's Place. And like the vampire Kiss she was now a part of, pack took care of its members.

Once outside in the sunshine, Pete felt as if she could breathe again. She closed her eyes and tilted her face up to the sun. The sigil moved slightly and she felt some of the leaves turn toward its rays. It's not as if she hated being in a closed office, but she much preferred to be outside, rain or shine, it didn't matter.

"Pete?"

She knew Shade was there watching her. She had even felt the pretty woman send her tiny jolts of comfort during the meeting inside. Pete just needed a moment.

"Yeah, Shade, I'm almost done. Don't you just love the sun? I think I'm going to take my bike and go for a really fast run before the day is out. Would you mind taking my bags back to the estate? Dominic is already ticked off at me, though I'm sure he'll be that way a lot if we stay together. I might as well get the—"

Shade cut her off. "Pete, did you really donate a million dollars to the Becca's Place?"

Pete turned to look at Shade. Now she was really embarrassed. She figured Shade had gotten the amount from someone in the room who knew about it too. "I never wanted anyone to find out. That's what anonymous donations are supposed to be, anonymous, you know? The money I got from the Mackey Corp. was sort of found money, something I hadn't counted on. The job I'd done for him was a community service thingy. I wasn't supposed to be paid. But when I fixed what I'd been told, I gave them some advice on a couple of other things too. The judge said it was all right that I take the money." She turned back to the sun. Pete found it easier to tell her the rest without looking at her right now. "I met the kids, Becca and Brent, once a long time ago. I was on call for a cable company then and a call came that the cable was down in that apartment. The kids watched me work on their cable while the mother lay on the couch comatose. The woman was so stoned that she didn't even realize I had taken them out of the house, fed them, and brought them back. We were gone for a good two or maybe three hours. She didn't notice her own kids missing, Shade. I could have been anyone! When I read about what happened to Becca in the paper a few months later, I was heartbroken for you and Brent. He's a great kid, by the way. So, in my own way, I'm helping little Becca when I didn't before."

Shade, crying, hugged Pete again, and Sara joined them for a group as they stood there on the busy sidewalk. Funny thing was, Pete was not at all embarrassed this time. She felt really good, and knew that she would have to take this job, if for no other reason than to help Shade and her house.

Chapter Eighteen

Dominic was waiting in the deserted kitchen for Pete when she returned. Her arms were loaded with shopping bags and there were still more in the car. The three of them had decided to celebrate Pete's job by doing some serious shopping.

Dominic didn't say a word, but stared at her for several seconds just taking her in. Then he scooped her up into his arms, threw her over his shoulder, and took packages and all down to what he now considered their bedroom. She didn't say anything to him as everything passed by them in a blur upside down.

"You'd better have a good reason for —"

Dominic didn't let her get any further, as his mouth covered hers in a devastating kiss. He simply held her close to his body, hugging her, needing her touch as he needed anything else. He pulled back slightly, looked in her eyes, and felt humbled by what he saw there.

"I sorry, so very sorry. I missed you. I was an ass, an overbearing, arrogant ass."

Dominic had had most of the day to think about what he had demanded of Pete, and what she had said in return. When he had tried to contact her several times throughout the day, he met with resistance. Even their bond was blocked from him communicating with her. It was then that he decided that he could not—no, he would not demand and dictate to her again. She was too stubborn and too strong to piss off without pain. And he had been in pain all day.

"Me too, Dominic. I have to tell you something. I...I love you. But I don't want anyone in my life who feels that I'm too stupid to make decisions on my own. I took precautions before I left the house this morning, and that's why I asked Sara and Shade to go with me. Of course I had to pay a price; they took me shopping for clothes. But I can't live with you if I have to worry that every time I make a decision, I have to worry about how you will react. Understand?"

"Shopping? Like shopping for the nice little number you teased me with today shopping? And by the way, that was the worst kind of cruel, letting me see you all decked out, and then wiping it out. Cruel, baby, that was just cruel. Let's look at what you have here; maybe you could give me a fashion show."

He looked at the names on the bags and felt his cock harden. Oh yeah, there was definitely going to be some modeling tonight.

"Focus, you baboon. I'm talking about our future together. Will you put that down and listen to me?"

He continued pulling out item after tiny item. The colors alone were erotic enough to have his cock harden more, but the sets, both top and bottoms, being so tiny and so...lacy had his mouth watering and the thought of it being next to her skin, his hands pulling them off her, tasting what he revealed when he ripped them from her...Christ, he was not going to last long once he had her beneath him, he thought. He stopped his plundering, looked at her, and smiled.

"I'm not a baboon, but I do love you. I will try and I mean really try, not to piss you off again by being an 'arrogant ass,' as you so eloquently put it. All right? Now, go put this on. I wanna rip it from your delicious body." He handed her the skimpiest garments in the bag.

"No more ripping. This stuff is expensive! Oh yeah, I have a job I need to tell you about."

"Later, baby, tell me later. And I'll rip and replace, how's that sound? You know you love it when I get all caveman-ish."

He watched as she looked at the green pieces in her hand then back to his face. Her eyes had turned to shimmering silver and glowed with need. His own eyes had turned as well; red haze surrounded her. He ran his tongue along his teeth as he felt his fangs lengthen and stretch. "Hurry," was all he said, and she bolted to the bathroom. She would be lucky if he didn't need to replace all of the purchases before sunrise at this rate. And he was waiting by the door, naked and ready for her, when she came out dressed as he had requested.

~~~

"I've been looking over your list about your brothers, Pete, and I must say again how very well put together it is. Anyway, I think that you may have overestimated their abilities a little. I would say that their power is based on black magic, as you have stated, but they don't have much in the way of natural talent. And in the magical world, that is very important."

James and Savannah had worked on the list for most of the day. And they had both decided that based on what they had witnessed the day before; Pete was much stronger than all of her brothers put together. Her talent was the combination of both parents having natural magick, even if one of them was using black at the time.

"But I thought that black magic was extremely powerful, and that the more one used it, the stronger that person became. At least that's what it seemed like when I was living with them. My brother Zeus could shift into a bird of prey, I think it was a falcon. He couldn't hold it for very long, maybe a couple of hours at the most. Then Heph could teleport, again not far, maybe ten miles at a time and as far away as he'd ever gotten was maybe fifty miles before he'd had to call Mother and have her come and get him. And if any of them used any of the extreme stuff, they would be down for a couple of hours. Depending on the amount of time it was used it could be a couple of days."

"Your brother Heph, you mean as in Hephaestus the god of fire? Your mother named your brothers after Greek gods? Well, she certainly had a very high opinion of her breeding capabilities, didn't she? You have to tell me all of their names. This is just too good not to investigate more closely. When you listed them on the sheet, you didn't put their birth names, just nick names. Why not?"

James did not have many names in his "Big Book of Beings," as he had titled it, so she had not thought to do it any differently than he had.

"Not just the gods, but the Olympians as well so their names are Apollo, Ares, Hephaestus, or Heph for short, Hermes, Cronus and Zeus, and that's in order of birth. I don't know the last one's name, but it's probably Hades or Poseidon or something equally stupid. You didn't list the names in your journal; I figured it was because of some power it gave you if you had their name. I guess I was sort of thinking like Rumplestiltskin, where his name meant power to the one who knew it." She blushed.

"But your name, it's not a god or an Olympian. What kind of name is Piccadilly?" Savannah asked her.

"I'm not named after a 'whom' but a 'what.' The Piccadilly Inn in Fresno California. She claims that's where I was conceived. Probably behind the place rather than inside of it, if her track record is any indication, and I have every doubt she had a room there. So my name is Piccadilly Fresno Bartholomew. My brother Apollo started calling me Dilly Bar when I was about three, I guess, and it stuck. I changed it to Pete because it was so far from both my real and their nick name that it felt good." She shrugged, thinking that if she never heard the name Dilly again, she would be very happy.

"What an unfortunate name, but Pete is nice. I must say that Pete suits you much better than Piccadilly. And that's a good theory about the little man and his name, I like it. But it was simply a matter of not being able to pronounce their names in a language we would be able to understand, not to mention spell. Why, one gnome's name was Peellalitamanishundish. He liked to be called Fred if you can believe that. Gnomes can be incredibly stupid. But Fred was very polite. I liked him," Elizabeth told her as she joined the group, Mel close behind.

As always, they were in the kitchen, and Dunc and Penny were making large sandwiches and pouring drinks.

"You're making that up! Peelatitdasastupidname, or whatever it was, being called Fred. Mother, you need serious help." But they all got a good laugh out of it.

Mel kissed her mother's cheek. Pete watched the family interact with each other, Dunc and Penny fuss over them all. Had someone told her that she would be sitting in a room full of vampires and having fun, she would have probably laughed at them. Yet, here she sat.

"Back to your brothers. Yes, they are strong, but black magic isn't a renewable resource like your magic is. Black magic, or tainted magic, only works through spells and potions. Also, it takes from the earth as a whole. The user needs to keep taking and taking and sometimes resorting to theft to keep up their appearances of being strong. White magic, or pure magic, on the other hand, borrows, much like the bargain you set up before you helped Sara. You made a fair trade where you both exchanged something that had value or worth only to you. I would image that you might have known that naturally, instinctually, because of the purity of your heart."

Pete flushed. She didn't know how she knew to do that, he was right. But him telling her that her heart was pure...well, hardly. She had plenty of bad thoughts.

"Your magic is also pure. In the sense that it borrows, not steals from the elements around you like black does. But people who steal and steal what they use and not give back will only burn out eventually. Or have it turn back on them. The power of magic is always the same for both dark and white magic; it returns tenfold. What you take must be returned unto the lender ten times to whatever extent of resources you use," James explained to her, looking up notes in his book as he did.

"So how do I beat them? Because I will not go back with them to be their breeder, or anything else they might have in mind," she told the room in general.

Pete had been practicing her magic with Queenie all evening after they had returned from shopping. While Pete was getting stronger, she did not know if she could take on her family and defeat them.

"The only person you are going to be breeding for is me, woman. And it won't be just you trying to beat them. We'll all be there for you, with you."

She looked over at Dominic and smiled. The thought of spending eternity with him simply made her toes curl. She felt him move through her and smiled again at the images he sent to her by their special connection. She suddenly wondered if eternity was going to be long enough. Daniel Taggert came into the room just as Dominic was finished talking.

Pete and Daniel had just completed the security changes that Pete had suggested yesterday. The changes were simple but very effective. The system could not be cut into without triggering several others and it was nearly impossible to disable the gate surrounding the mansion by cutting into the electrical wiring because they had rigged the harness to overlap at random junctures, sometimes going for several sections together. It could go for several sections before it had its own grid, or several miles. Keeping electricity going to the areas was a major problem with this much equipment running. If the power were cut to the house and the security camera, normally one would not be able to see anything.

However, with the system they had installed, this was no longer a problem. They had had the cables dropped off and with the help of a couple of weres at the power plant, they had the power grid turned off long enough to work on it without a lot of others knowing anything about what they were doing. That was the thing about covert security, the more people who knew about it, the less effective it became.

"They're here," Daniel said with a grin. "They arrived in town about twenty minutes ago. They are staying at that inn on Market Avenue. Their car, surprise, surprise, is a total piece of crap and probably won't take them back to their home, at least not without a major overhaul. So for them to confront you, they'll need to walk here, teleport, or take a cab. Jim, the owner of the inn, would probably believe they'd hitch a ride, that's how stupid they are. He said that he had to explain to them eight times that they couldn't each have a room as the inn only had four rooms total and two of them were already occupied. When he told them he would not kick the other two couples out, they told him he should have more respect for his betters. Then proceed to tell him how he should have special rooms set up for special guests like them at all times."

"Better than what is what I'd like to know. Did they say anything else?" Pete was almost afraid to hear what he'd say next.

"Nah, not really. Said they were here to pick up their long lost sister and take her home with them. Oh yeah, and you're nuts," he told her with a cocky grin.

"Excuse me? What do you mean I'm nuts?" She waited for him to explain while he got a large roast beef sub off the seemingly never empty tray Dunc had brought in.

"Yeah, it seems they've got a court order saying that you need constant care and that you are incapable of making any decisions on your own. That a woman by the name of, get this, Aphrodite is your legal guardian. Now if I were the judge and heard all of those names together, I'd have all of them committed, not you. Aphrodite, isn't she some sort of god of dirt or something?" If Daniel had not been so helpful, she might have gotten up and smacked him.

"She's the goddess of love and she's my mother — Aphrodite, not my mother. Who the hell would give them a court order? What the hell am I supposed to do now? Every cop in town knows who I am. Shit! I won't be able to move without someone trying to arrest me and to hand me over. I wonder if the stupid woman remembers that I took care of her more than she did me when I lived at home."

"They won't be able to get you here, love. And I've talked with Bradley. It seems he has a brother and a few other pack members on the local force; they know to keep you safe. But that doesn't solve our problem. They are still going to be out there waiting. They can't leave because of their transportation issues, and as you have pointed out, I don't think that they'll leave without you at any rate. You've become the sole reason for their woes of late, I imagine. We'll need to decide to either confront them or ignore them. Pete, you know them better than any of us. What do you think we should do?"

Aaron looked directly at her and no one else. He was saying, "your decision, kid," and she knew it.

She knew that there was no point in saying that it was not anyone's problem but her own, that they were her blood relatives, not theirs. But Aaron's Kiss had taken her in as one of their own, and nothing she could say would change their minds. She looked around the room and realized that she was one of theirs, a friend, and a lover. Aaron and Sara had opened their home to her, Colin and Shade gave her friendship and understanding, and Dominic loved her. They had let her into their hearts and she had never had anyone be so open, friendly, or helpful to her before. She was a part of something.

"I know this sounds so inadequate, but I wanted to say thank you to all of you. You can't know how much it means to me, how much all of you have come mean to me. I...I think—"

Duncan walked into the big room and made a grave announcement before she could finish.

"Miss Pete, there is an objectionable personage at the front gate who is demanding entrance. He is claiming to be one of your guardians and is here to 'fetch' you home. What would you like me to do to him?"

Chapter Nineteen

Pete laughed even as she felt like crying. Dunc had become her newest champion, it seemed. She looked to Aaron, as it was his home, and silently asked him to make the decision. The children had already been taken to the Keep earlier that day, and already had nearly all of the royal court, including the guards, wrapped around their little fingers, so she was no longer worried about them.

"Dunc, my man, allow this person in. Daniel, could you please alert the pack members and let them know the faction has arrived finally? Pete, nothing will happen today. He's here only to see if he can persuade you to come with him without a fight, which I'm betting he fully expects, as he has come alone. Dominic, let's go and greet the rabble with your mate, shall we?" When she walked out of the front doors, she was flanked by both men.

~~~

Pete watched as Ares was just getting out of the car. The low, mean growl behind him had him turning quickly. Right behind him was a pack of wolves not ten feet away. He pressed his back against the car door and did not move. Pete was sure he was not stupid enough to take on a dozen full grown wolves and believe he would come out on top. And

Ares had always managed to come out on top, no matter who he had to kill to get there.

The largest wolf by a good forty pounds of pure muscle moved closer to the car, raised his hackles, and bared his teeth. When he moved to within a foot of Ares, he lifted his hind leg and pissed all over him. Ares started to move forward to challenge the wolf, she thought, to make him pay for ruining his clothes, but stopped, frozen as the entire pack moved three steps forward, teeth bared and growling menacingly at him. Their growls were a harmony of sounds and tones that seemed to reverberate around them all as they moved forward toward her brother.

The feelings running through him were just what his victims had felt when faced with him or one of her brothers. Of course, this would never have occurred to him, just as it would not have to any of the others. Pete could feel his terror, taste it even. She waited until he turned to look at her before she spoke.

"I wouldn't, if I were you. Run, I mean. I'd stay very still and make no sudden moves. I've learned that they don't care for food that doesn't make them work for it. Maybe they'll kill you quickly and you won't be alive when they eat you. Or if you'd like, you can run. That will certainly make them happy, running you down, chewing on your soft tissue before breaking bones. You know, on second thought, I want you to run. Yes, please run from them. I believe I'd like that very much."

As soon as she spoke, Bradley walked over to her and sat to her right. She reached down and scratched him behind the ears. She realized then that he had been the one who had peed all over Ares. She smiled. Leaning down, she spoke in a voice everyone could hear and said, "Good boy."

Dominic walked up behind her, put his arms around her waist, and pulled her into his body. He was clearly showing ownership of her, and normally that would bother her, but she found that she needed his touch more than anything at that moment and leaned back against him. Aaron flanked her on her other side as the wolves fanned out around her and the men.

"Are they gonna eat me, Dilly Bar?"

Ares' voice sounded a little higher than he would normally speak to her or anyone he had thought to dominate and she found she enjoyed that tremor in his voice.

"I'm not sure yet what I want them to do to you. I haven't decided. What do you want? If your answer isn't too offensive, then I might let you live, human. And be quick about it. I have better things to do than to stand around with a fool who comes to my home unannounced."

Aaron, fangs bared and eyes glowing a deep blood red, stepped up beside Ares using the speed of his kind. Pete smiled broadly when she heard Ares whimper.

"I have a court order that states that Dilly Bar, err Piccadilly, my sister, is crazy. Well, it says that she is unbalanced, and suffering from hallucinations and delusions of grandeur. That she is unfit to be left alone. My mother has been named her guardian; I'm here to take her home, back home with me, us."

Ares pulled the paper out of his jacket and shakily handed it over to Aaron. He looked at Pete with a questioning brow. At her nod, he opened it and began to read it.

"Pete, my dear, are you having delusions of grandeur again? My, my, and all this time we thought you to be the real deal." He turned to look back at her brother. "She isn't left alone. As you can see, she has quite a few beings around her at all times. Dominic, why don't you bring your lovely wife around so she can introduce us to her, hummm...brother?"

Pete heard the way Aaron had emphasized the word "being," but she doubted that Ares had. She could see that he was sure of what the outcome of today's meeting was going to be and that Ares had missed the small enounce. Pete wondered if her family had ever been told no before.

She and Dominic walked to just beside Aaron, and the wolves had moved just enough to allow them a clear view of the human. None of them would let her get close enough for Ares to be able to touch her, yet close enough for him to see. Bradley, still in wolf form, had followed her and again sat, this time in front of her.

"Sire, Dominic, this is one of my brothers, Ares Bartholomew. Ares, this is my master, Aaron MacManus, and my mate, Dominic Marshall. And this is my alpha, Bradley, master of this pack. You are trespassing here and are not welcome, so what the fuck do you want?"

Pete had been very careful to keep her powers in check. Sara warned her that there was no reason to give them any more information about her and her powers than necessary. Sara was helping her hold them; hide them really until the time came when Pete would need to confront the brothers. There was no doubt that she would have to, and having the upper hand could save her life.

"Can you call off your dogs and let's be civil about this?"

He stiffened up again as the alpha stood up on his hind legs and moved, bracing himself on the car very close to where Ares was. He growled deep in his throat at him.

"He's not a dog, you moronic fuck. He's a wolf. And you'd do well to remember that. Dog indeed! Do you realize he could snap your scrawny neck in a second if I wanted him

190

to? I wonder why I didn't realize you were this stupid when I lived at home. Now, what do you want?"

Bradley growled again, as if begging for her to ask him to kill the man. Pete was very close to saying have a good meal. She might have, too, if she wasn't afraid Bradley and the others would be sick from him. Just the thought of Ares being eaten by the pack made her smile. She wondered fleetingly if she was as bad as them. No, she thought, she only thought it. They actually carried through with it.

Ares didn't like Pete being smart with him. She could tell by the stiffening of his body. So when Ares leapt forward suddenly and grabbed her arm and meant to strike her, Dominic had him by the neck and dangling from the ground a good two feet before he could draw back his other hand to hit her. Pete had been so startled by both of the men that she did not move for several seconds. And she did not know how much longer she would have stood there if Dominic hadn't spoken just when he had.

"Touch her again and I will kill you, you fucking worthless excuse for a human being. I will kill you in ways that will make what you've been up to seem like child's play. Trust me when I say I have a great deal more practice and I'm much more patient with bloodletting."

The intimidation and menace in voice was powerful, leaving Ares no doubt of the man's claim, Pete was sure. Then Dominic licked her brother, a long swipe of his tongue along his jugular.

"You will get into that piece of a shit car, turn it around, and never come near her again, or I swear to you that nothing will keep me from you. Do I make myself perfectly clear?" To make sure he understood, Dominic shook him hard again, and then dropped him to the ground. Pete laughed when she realized that Ares had wet himself.

~~~

Ares got into his car very slowly, as the pack had not backed away when the others had reentered the house, but had moved closer and were now baring their teeth and had unsheathed their claws.

The car had been giving them problems all the way there so when it did not start on the first two tries, Ares was not surprised. When he was finally able to start it and turn the car around and head back toward the front gate of the estate, he was relieved to see his escort, the pack, Pete had called them, start to fall away a few at a time, and by the time he reached the iron gates, only four followed. He didn't even pause, afraid that one or all of them would make him very sorry he had. He drove straight out the gate and to the relative safety of the main road.

Ares had to think. Things were not going as Sherman or their mother had said they would. Not only was Pete not the weakling they had thought she would be, but she had a very large, very strong husband as well.

The car was running badly, they were nearly broke, and they had no one to steal anything from. This was all Dilly's fault, he thought. If she would just learn her place and come back with them, everything would be fine again, he was sure of it. And then Ares could go on with his own plan. He was not sure what to tell Sherman and the rest about what had happened. He knew their master and his older brother would be angry.

They had thought that by sending Ares alone, it would be enough to bring her home without any problems. No one had figured she would have a husband, and what was it with the whole "master" thing? And those dogs. She had called them wolves. She had a pack of wolves at her disposal.

By the time Ares had gotten back to the dingy hotel, he had convinced himself that he had put up a good fight and that it was not his fault that they had attacked him without provocation because he had wanted to bring his poor sister home. Dilly was going to have to pay, that much he was sure of. She was going to pay like no one who had ever crossed him had. He was just not sure how much Sherman was going to make him pay for her not being with him now.

"What do you mean she's changed? Changed how? Her clothes? Her hair style? What? Telling me that she is different does not explain why you don't have her yet." Apollo was not just mad, but furious at him. And Sherman was not happy either. Ares just wanted to get out of this fucking town as soon as possible; there was something not right about it and the people in it, damn it.

"She has this tattoo now. It covers her face and neck and I swear to Christ, it moved. And I could feel this strange vibe from those men too. Nothing like I've felt before. I know they were fucking vamps, but they had a, I don't know, a power with them. And it was fucking strong. I don't understand it, Mother. You said she'd be a weakling, no problems at all, that after all this time she'd beg us to take her home."

"She just needs to see we mean business. Once we get back there and combine our forces, she'll fold. That's the way she's always done it. And without me to guide her, she won't have any clue how to use the little bit of white magic she had. You'll see. Dilly will see reason."

Ares just looked at his mother. Christ, he couldn't wait for the stupid bitch to die. A few more doses of the poison he'd been feeding her and he would be in charge. Fucking cunt. They didn't need her anymore anyway.

"Well, that ain't right either," Ares continued. "Her voice sounded strong, and like she didn't give a shit if those dogs ate me or not. No, they weren't dogs, she'd told me, but wolves. How the fuck did she know they were wolves and how do you even get a pack of them trained to help you? And those freaky vamps?"

Ares had heard of them before, of course. With someone like Sherman helping them, they couldn't help but learn of the different kinds of beings. But those had been the first ones he had ever encountered. He knew as soon as he could he was gonna stake that big one and watch as the sun turned him to French fries. Yeah, he was gonna enjoy that one dying.

"This tattoo, you said it covered her face? How much of it? These are details you should have gotten, Ares. You had a cell phone. Why didn't you just snap a picture of it for us? Shit, if I'd of known you were gonna fuck it up so badly, I'd have gone myself," Sherman said with disgust. At that moment, Ares hated the man.

Sherman paced the small room, barely looking where he set his feet. The man had power, no doubt about that. It practically shimmered off him. And knowledge…Sherman seemed to know everything about everything. He had first approached them when Dilly had turned six. He never helped her, saying that she was too immature for their kind of lessons, but had spent countless hours with them — more so in the past year.

Did the man actually think that Ares could have reached into his pants pocket and said, "Hold for me, sis. I'm sure Mom will be so happy for a picture of the two of us together"?

His mom had been bitching about Dilly's tat since Ares had mentioned it upon his return. He wished any of them had of gone to get her and not him. They all could have gone after her for all he cared. Then one of them could have piss all over himself.

"Well, we'll have to get her and that is all there is to it. I want her and I mean to have her, husband or not. I don't give a shit what she's changed into; she's not anything close to what I am. As the oldest, I claim the right to breed a child from her. Then if she's smart enough to keep her mouth shut, I won't need to kill her once I have my child," Apollo announced smugly.

Sherman just smiled at him. Ares shuddered at what he thought the smile could mean. It could have meant, "Yes, you will have a child with her," or, "You just keep on dreaming, little boy. It is I who will be fucking her until she is with my child." Ares thought it was the latter of the two and shuddered again. He could almost feel sorry for his little sister. Almost.

Ares left the room thinking he wished they had stayed home. He had a plan of his own and it didn't include Dilly having a child of Apollo's or Sherman's. He was going to breed Dilly as much as he could. He was planning on breeding powerful children from her then killing her. But first, he thought, he was going to kill his brothers and absorb their powers.

That to him was the greatest power about the type of magic they used. It could be taken from someone you killed and it became yours, adding to and strengthening your own. Yeah, Apollo, you try and take what's mine, he thought again.

Ares went to the storage unit they had spent their last thirty bucks on, opened the door quietly, and shut it that way as well. The man hanging from the middle was still alive. Good, he thought, more fun for him.

Ares had enjoyed the man the other night. They all had, actually. Ares thought the man hanging before him had proven to be quite the diversion in an otherwise boring trip. Opening his pants, he began to fist his cock hard, stroking it as he neared the man. He liked the torture more than the power it gave him sometimes. Then fucking his prey while they lay dying gave him a rush like nothing ever had. His cock hardened more as he thought about pounding hard into the dying man. He thought about the screams, the blood, and nearly came. We cannot have that, he thought with a sadistic grin, and moved in front of the man.

Grabbing the man at both hips, he rubbed his cock over his prey's soft one. Powerless, the prey whimpered and mewed at Ares. His cock jerked in response.

"I'm going to fuck you again. Fuck you until my cum fills your ass. Fuck you until I'm raw. Will you like that, prey?" Ares' voice was soft and low, menacing and loving.

Turning Prey around, Ares lifted him slightly and rammed his cock into him. He was not as tight as he had been before, but Prey still gripped his cock. Pulling the knife out of his back sheath, he pumped into the tiny hole again and was rewarded with blood oozing from the opening and around Ares' cock. He pumped harder and as soon as his balls tightened and he was ready to come, he slammed the knife into Prey's heart and killed him. Even as he died, Ares emptied himself in him.

Sated now, he decided he was going to have to find him someone again soon, maybe two this time.

The seven men and one woman sat up nearly all night, plotting and planning how to get to Dilly. However, the opportunity to get to her came a lot sooner than they thought and in a way they had not expected.

CHAPTER TWENTY

"I have to go to Becca's Place this morning. I have a crew of men coming out and I need to get them started on the security and computer wiring," Pete explained to Dominic.

He was driving her crazy and if she did not get away from him soon, she was going to scream. He had been following her around for two days and she needed to have some alone time. She was not used to having someone breathing down her neck all the flipping time.

"I'll come with you. And if it runs into later in the afternoon, we'll sleep at Colin and Shade's house. I don't want you to go out alone, Pete. I know you think that sounds possessive. Then that's what I am. I can't help it where you're concerned." He tried to soften it with a silly grin, but she saw through it.

"Dominic, there are a dozen pack members already going to be there milling around and Bradley himself wants to 'hang around' to watch how things are done. I'm not going to go anywhere but to there and back."

Pete had had this same argument with him for two days. Enough was enough already. Her brothers had not come back, nor had they made any kind of effort to contact her.

She had hoped that they had given up and were getting ready to leave again.

"Well, let's get going. What're you waiting for?" He was going with her and that was that, she thought with a groan. Well, fuck a duck and watch it waddle.

An hour just before sunset, they pulled up in front of the big, newly constructed house. It was deceptively small from the outside. When finished, it would be able to care for twenty-four children. There would be a dining hall, library, and medical facility as well. The whole place would be wired with interior and exterior security surveillance equipment. They had decided to wire the house separate from the main house, but still have the capability of seeing either property from the security tower that would be manned twenty-four/seven by an armed guard. Pete was there today to set up and install some of the cameras in the bedrooms and halls on the second and third floors so they could finish the dry wall application as soon as she was finished.

"Eon, can you take this cable back down to the kitchen and bring up the heavier gauge? This isn't strong enough to carry the juice I need."

Pete was using as many weres and vamps as she could. What they lacked in experience, they more than made up for in muscle and willingness to work hard. Also, the fewer humans who knew about the inner workings of the systems she was installing, the better. The campus was catering to any child that needed protection and a safe haven. The setup had to be perfect.

When Eon returned with the cables, he was with two other young wolves. He had told her yesterday that he had had a talk with Bradley and that he had been invited to stay with them at the pack house. Eon had also explained, although not in great detail, that the talk had taught him a few things about was happening to his body that he'd been "totally freaked" about. Bradley had assured him that he would also be safe from his mother. Pete thought that Eon was happier about that more than anything else.

Eon had explained that Bradley was going to be harder on him than Pete had been about his education and he would be going to college as well as finish up his high school, "or else." She didn't ask what that might mean, but the look of terror on her friend's face said enough.

"Pete, do you care if we knock off early tonight? The guys and I wanna catch a movie at the pack house. They have this state of the art movie system that you wouldn't believe. And more food than I can eat in one sitting."

"Yeah, sure, just make sure you tell Bradley or Dominic that you're leaving, okay? Don't want them to freak out again."

"That's for sure. Are they still pissed about it, you think?"

When they had arrived this morning, she had sent Eon and a couple of others into town to grab some donuts and coffee for everyone. When Dominic realized that she had been left alone on the third floor, he and Bradley had had a fit! They seemed to forget that there were about twenty other people on the floor below her and several dozen more around the grounds. They had told these men to stick to her like glue, and they had not. It had taken about an hour to calm the two men down and longer still to get the younger wolves to feel safe from them.

"They're fine. Have you seen either of them lately? I thought they were going to the tower to see if the line of sight was all right." She looked at her watch and realized it had been about an hour. She knew that Dominic would have to go to ground soon.

"Nope. Want I should go look for them? And this is me hoping you'll say no. I don't think I wanna be around either of them for a couple of days."

She knew he would go if she said yes, but what was the point? Plus, she had some quiet time for the first time in days.

"Nah, they'll show up soon. We'll have to call it a day soon anyway." She reached out to Dominic and could not reach him; something was blocking her path. She didn't really think on it too much, and continued wiring the last bedroom.

She had just reached the lower floor when she felt something akin to terror race through her, leaving her weak and out of breath, then...nothing. She reached out to Dominic again and felt a small but weak link to him. Stretching harder, she could feel his pain and weakness. Something had happened, something bad, and he was losing blood. She looked up and realized how late it was and was suddenly worried about him and the sun.

"Dominic?" She found herself racing across the lawn toward the main house before she realized it. Shade was just coming out and met her on the main path to the house with a tray of drinks. She suddenly dropped them and ran toward her until they met on the path.

"What is it, Pete? I felt your pain. What's happened?"

"Dominic, something has happened to Dominic. Please tell me he is with Colin. He was with Bradley earlier and they left to go to the tower. I felt his pain then nothing. I have to find him, Shade! Oh God, what if my brothers have him?"

"We have to wake Colin, and get in touch with the pack to see if they've heard from them, or if Bradley is with them. Come on, I'll contact Sara and have her and Aaron come here too."

An hour later, they were contacted by Hermes, one of Pete's other brothers. They had both men. He said and was willing to trade them if she came along quietly and she "left her fucking dogs at home."

"Where are they, you worthless piece of shit? I swear if you've hurt them, I won't rest until I strip every inch of skin from your body piece by little piece."

"And here we all thought you didn't have the stomach to be one of us. You'll do as you're told, do you hear me? I'm not the pussy you think I am. I'd rather just kill you and end this stupidity, but Apollo wants you for his own reasons, and he's the oldest. Sherman knows what he's about, and he knows just how to make them suffer in ways you can't even think of. Now, you'll come to that baseball field in the center of town at sunset, and you'll come alone. If I even smell one dog, or feel any other power other than ours, I'll kill them both after I kill you."

"I'll be there, but you'd better be prepared, Hermes, all of you, because I'm only going to ask you the one time to walk away or I'm going to kill you all. You can bank on that." Pete hung up the phone, tears in her eyes. "They're going to kill them anyway, aren't they?"

"Not if I fucking have anything to say about it," Mel said as she hugged Pete to her. "That man has caused enough problems for several lifetimes and this will end now."

Mel had told Pete that while she couldn't use her magic against them because it wasn't fated that she interfere, she could be support for them and guide them. The Fates, or the Sisters Three, were very particular about that.

~~~

They had thought to stake Dominic out in the sun and just let him fry to show her they meant business, but Sherman had pointed out that with him alive, they had a bargaining chip against the others if Dilly brought them with her. He said that once they got her home and the other vamps gave up looking for her, then they could do whatever they wanted to her husband, which meant they were planning to torture him. As for the dog, they didn't know what Bradley was other than that Pete had called him a wolf, but he would prove to be a fun toy once they were back home. With Sherman's magic gone, the magic that had once made him a true immortal, he could not tell what a species was until he tasted them. And he did not want to bite Bradley to see how much power the man had.

Ares had decided to keep Bradley for himself. His plan was to make him pay for pissing on him, at least until the wolf's heart gave out under the stress and pain. Ares had a large arsenal of torture devices.

The trap had been to wait for them to come out and feed, or whatever the dog did, and drop silver chains onto them as they were walking through the field. Silver had the same effect on both of the beings, rendering them helpless and in a great deal of pain as it seared itself into their flesh. Hermes and Pan, Pete's youngest brother, had caught Dominic and Bradley unawares when the two men had been on their way to the towers deep in the forest.

Once they were down, Pan had managed to get close enough to them to cut them in several places with the silver tipped blades that Sherman had provided. He told them that the blades were specially enhanced and that silver dust would stay in the wound, eating away at the flesh as long as the men did not get to feed and break the magic. Once they were subdued and weak enough, it was little problem to load them into the van they had stolen and take them to the field.

CHAPTER TWENTY-ONE

"I don't like this and I forbid you to go out there alone. I am your master and I demand that you listen to me."

Aaron had been "demanding" of her for the better part of three hours and Pete still was not listening to him. It was his job to protect her, she understood that, but they had taken Dominic from her and they were going to pay. Besides, it was not as if she was going out alone. Sara and Shade both were helping her behind the lines so to speak. And Mel was going to be there, just not out in the open.

"Are all vampires this bossy?" Pete had turned to Sara when she asked, knowing full well the answer, but asking anyway to try and defuse some of her frustration.

"Yes they are, but I must agree with him, Pete. You are walking into a trap and you very well know it. I can keep them from knowing you're there until it's too late, but I don't want any of you hurt. Sherman is a very powerful being, as well as a heartless prick. I worry about your safety. You will be careful, won't you?"

"Yes. Queenie is going to be there too. She is as mad as a hornet right now and I think I like her that way. She said that if I got into trouble, she would make sure the men were safe and that she could help me by keeping me centered. I trust her."

As Pete drove along the road toward town, she felt the moon coming up. It felt like a pull on her skin and the Sigil on her body. The sudden need to feel it on her face was overwhelming, so overwhelming that she pulled over to the side of the road and took off her helmet. She raised her face to the moon's light in much the same way she had with the sun light when she had been standing outside the Mackey building only a few days ago. It felt just as good, so good in fact that she took off her flannel shirt and t-shirt and stood there in her skimpy bra, her head back while she absorbed the power from the lunar rays.

Pete felt the first stirring of the leaves after a couple seconds of standing there. Then the longer she stood there, the more she could feel their reaction to the lunar pull. It was believed of all magical beings that the moon had a better healing process and stronger properties than the sun, especially to plants and herbs. When a plant seemed to be reaching for the sun, it was in actuality reaching for the moon.

Pete's body was soon pulsing with energy and power. She felt the ivy tighten around her bicep and thigh, only to realize that it was not just tightening but the muscles there were becoming stronger and more defined, making the vine feel too small. The vine moving to accommodate this change had it shifting along her body in a dance of a caress, moving and shaping itself to her newer body.

Her spine tingled at first with strength, the muscles in her back elongating and becoming more flexible and stronger. The magic of the vines moved down along her arms and through her waist and abs. The power they gave off was more defined, more shieldlike than before. It was as though it knew it needed to prepare her for battle. She removed her bra when she felt the leaves move up and cup her breasts protectively, shielding her nudity and protecting her heart. The vine that was along her spine stretched and pulled until it covered her thighs and the calves of her legs. Long lines of branches encircled her ankles and strengthened her knees. The movement along her arms had her watching in wonder as her elbows and wrists were protected like her knees, sheathed in a heavy branch and armored with leaves. Her body was encased now, safe from whatever they threw at her, strengthened by the protective shell around her.

When she finally reached the field where they were waiting, she felt more powerful than she had ever been. Strength and confidence radiated from her in arcs of light and pulses of unspent energy all over her body. She walked to the group of them as if she didn't have a care in the world.

"Hello, Mother, it's been a long time. Too bad it couldn't have been longer. You must be my youngest brother, I'm Pete. I'm sorry to say that I'm not at all happy to meet you." Turning to the others, she said, "I will give you this one chance to tell me where they are and to leave here and never to return, any of you. I don't want to have to kill you all, but I will. I can."

She watched as Sherman took two steps away from the group. He would run, she thought, but he could not hide. He was as dead at the others.

"You try, sister dear, and he dies," Apollo said calmly. "It's as simple as that. You think you're so strong? Well, you aren't half the power base we are. Now, this is what's going to happen. We're all going to get into the car and pretend this never happened."

She felt him then; Dominic was close. Opening herself up to him was not as hard as she had thought it would be.

He was hurt and extremely weak. Silver. She could almost taste it on him; it felt as if it was inside of him. Bradley was there, too, but not as weak as Dominic. She sent a message to his brother, David, and to Aaron telling them she had found them and where to look. And she told them to please hurry, that both of them were weak.

"Baby, I'm here. I'm all right; go get Aaron and the others. These men are too dangerous for you to take on alone."

It took her a few seconds to realize he was actually telling her to leave him there and send someone else to come back for him. She was going to kill him if he lived through this.

"Shut up, you ass. I can feel your pain and your loss of blood. Send someone back for you; is that what you're saying? Are you insane? No, don't answer that. You'll just piss me off more than you already have. You have to trust me, and do as I say. I contacted Bradley's family and Aaron, and they'll be here soon. I need for both of you to dig your feet and hands into the soil under you. Shade is going to have the earth try and heal you enough to get us out of here."

She hated to do it, but she closed off the connection to the men so that she could concentrate on the people in front of her.

Shade had a special connection with the earth. Her power was of the elements, just like Pete's. But where Pete could only ask help from the under earth part of the elements, Shade could ask the above earth as well. Shade had once healed Brent when he was near death by asking the earth to heal him by bringing him into the ground. Poor guy had been drugged by his own mother and used as bait to lure both Sara and Shade to a cave to be killed. These two would be just as safe with Shade helping.

"Oh Pete, you are so stupid if you think that we are not prepared for you and your little display of lights. It is pretty, as you are well aware, but it will not stop me. I mean to have you, my dear. I'll have you over and over again until I tire of you. Then maybe I'll give you to your brothers as their reward. Your mother, bless her, has given you to me. I will breed such powerful children from you, then we together will take my ex-mate down."

Pete glared at Sherman. "So be it. I have given you a bargain and you have refused it. You will now face me."

Suddenly, the earth shifted, knocking them slightly off their stance. Sherman was the quickest to recover and stood up. As she watched, he began making signs in the air and chanting something she could not hear. Ignoring him for the moment, she concentrated on her family. She knew that he was not going anywhere.

The first stirrings of fear showed in Apollo's eyes when Pete raised her hands toward him. Arches of light moved from her fingers and to the ground in front of her.

"Now, Dilly..." Aphrodite started condescendingly, as though Pete would never hurt her own mother.

Her mother's smug expression turned to horror as the first roots from the ground started to climb up her legs. Aphrodite moved to get away, stepping quickly and clumsily around the opening in the earth. As soon as she tripped, the weeds and grass began to cover her, tightening their grip every time she tried to break free. Within seconds, the greenery engulfed her, silencing her screams of terror as a long branch of a root stabbed into her mouth and out the back of her head, killing her.

The brothers stood frozen. They had not tried to reach their mother to save her. It had happened so quickly. In horror, they looked to Pete, and she smiled at them. She could smell the terror now.

While her mother's screams still echoed in Pete's ears, Zeus leapt forward to grab her. She sensed his need to kill her was more important than taking her home at this point. His own horrors at her made him act without thinking. It was a costly mistake on his part, deadly, as a matter of fact.

The moment Zeus touched her, his eyes widened in alarm, as though he finally realized he had made an error. A horrible, horrible error.

The vine, under Pete's command, reached out, grabbed his throat, and lifted him up off the ground. When he did not release her quick enough, another branch reached out, ripped his arm from the socket, and dropped it below him. Zeus watched as the ground lifted his appendage up and walked it over to a widening hole in the earth, end over end as it went. As he watched, screaming incoherently, the root around his neck pulled him closer to the same hole and dropped him into it. Within seconds, he, too, was completely sheathed in a cocoon. He made only one small noise. It sounded to Pete like a denial, a single "No."

Hermes and Pan moved toward where she knew Dominic and Bradley were being held. Pete's mind moved quickly to prevent them from using the two hostages as shields. The ground broke open at the brothers' feet. Roots and other undergrowth pulled them knee deep into a cavern.

"You'll not harm what is mine," she told them as she lifted her hands high in the air.

The first jolt of power hit her square in the chest, making her stagger slightly and barely able to keep her balance. Looking for the source, she watched as Sherman began gathering the elements around him again. Dark flashes of something, power, she supposed, began to fill the space between his hands.

Pete felt the magic, a cleaner, softer, but no less stronger magic seconds before she saw her. Suddenly, Queenie was standing next to her. Mel winked at Pete and smiled.

"He's mine. Take care of the rest. I will hold him for you."

Mel opened her hand and a single bolt of magic hit Sherman, knocking him back as his power dissipated. As Mel moved forward, her feet never touching the ground, Sherman began to crab walk backwards to get away from her. Pete smiled and looked at the remaining men.

A small root began making its way to the two men, encircling their throats in a loose rope around their neck. As it danced along the men, the grasses and roots below them started making their way up their bodies, stabbing them as it crawled up them, winding in and out of their bodies in a macabre art of stitching them together. When the roots were at their chests, the one at their throat began tightening them together, and squeezing them. Eyes protruded from their skulls, mouths opened, but no sound came forth. When the rope had worked so tight that it looked to be a part of their skin, it gave a final snap and both heads exploded from their bodies, eyes still open and staring at their bodies before they, too, fell into the earth.

Cronus turned and ran toward the outfield of the park. A pack of wolves waiting in the dark overpowered him, taking him to the ground even as he looked back at the others. David, Pete thought, the brother of the alpha, ripped out his throat before Cronus hit the ground. The wolves feasted on his blood and the fresh meat of the kill. As one, they raised their bloodied faces to the moon and howled. It seemed as though revenge had never tasted so sweet to them. Hephaestus screamed as he watched in horror while the pack shredded and tore at his brother's still-warm flesh.

Pete knew Cronus had not been dead when the wolves had started eating and tearing at him. As Cronus lay bleeding, she could hear his screams over Hephaestus's.

Hephaestus turned back to Apollo and Pete and abruptly stopped screaming. His smile, in the heavy, deafening silence was eerie and frightening to her. He continued to smile as he reached behind him and pulled a gun out of his back. Instead of pointing it at Pete, as she had fully expected him to do, he put it to his own head and pulled the trigger, letting her know he was not going out like the rest of the family. He was not going to wait to see what her powers had in store for him.

Turning to Apollo, she began to rise with the moving earth. As it mounded beneath her, lifting her far above her brother, the power of the earth filled her. The branches and vines moved forward and began to move toward him. When she had lifted enough, she raised her arms high above her and seemed to gather the forces of the night within her fingers. Eyes glowing bright and hard, she looked down at Apollo, said, "die," and sliced her hands to him, over him and through him.

He did not just come apart with her power, but exploded in pieces. Bone, blood, skin and organs spread out and over the ground, feeding it, nurturing it. And everywhere his blood touched, everything it fell upon, withered and died.

Mel still held Sherman in her coils of magic. He was bleeding and broken. Bones protruded from his arms and legs at odd angles, making him look like a horrid object of art. But she had not killed him.

"He is still my mate," Mel explained to Pete. "I can hold him, hurt him, but not kill him. I have failed you yet again, Piccadilly. I am so sorry. But I cannot finish him," Mel said with tears in her eyes.

"Look at the all powerful queen. You are nothing, you stupid bitch. When I'm free from this, I'll come back to you and I'll make you suffer for this. We aren't through yet. You'll see."

"Brave words for a dead man, wouldn't you say, Shade?" Sara said as she and Shade shimmered into sight beside the two women.

The power of them surged into Pete and then to Mel. Mel straightened and turned to the other two women who had joined them in the field.

"Yes, I would say he does try to pull off his bravado quite well. But he does need to go. Ladies, I don't know about any of you, but I believe it's a tad too chilly out here for this to go on. Besides, Pete has a mate to take care of. Pete, if you would be so kind, please take the trash out."

"You've made a fatal mistake taking what is mine, harming who I love, and hurting my friends. I gave you a chance, Sherman. I gave you more than you were going to offer me. Now you, too, must die." Pete had remained calm and stated her intentions without any emotions whatsoever. "Your death won't be quick, but painful and long. You're going to pay for what you've done; the punishment must meet the crimes."

"Don't feel sorry for me, bitch, and killing me won't be so easy. I am so much power you'll not pull me into your trap."

Before he could gather whatever he could, Shade grabbed him with her power and threw him back, hurling him into the back fence at home plate. He lay there stunned for several seconds, more than enough time for Pete to rise and link hands with the women with her.

The four of them together knew no bounds. Their strength and power and, more than anything else, their friendship pulled together, making them a being to be reckoned with.

Shade called on the elements of her kind, the ground, the water, and beings inhabited within them. Before Sherman could get fully erect, he was being tossed to and fro and brought to face the four of them, his broken body a limp shadow of his former self. Shade held him there as though he were on trial.

Pete reached into the earth deeper than Shade had and lifted him up high above them, vines and roots wrapping around his legs and arms. Suddenly, a loud scream from him shattered the night when those roots began to pierce his skin at the pulse points on his body. Blood poured from those wounds, but even as the women watched, they could see that the vines began sucking the blackness out of him, pulling the evil from his body and into itself. The vines blackened and withered, but did not stop until the man who had once ruled beside the strongest being in any realm was nothing more than a shell, skin pulled tight over bones.

Sara, bringing forth her magic, pulled Sherman onto the ground and into the soft soil beneath him. As soon as his feet touched the earth, it closed over him and buried him to his knees. One vine, wrapped tightly around his chest, held Sherman upright until the ground became tight and compacted around him. When he was tightly bound, it slithered away and beneath the dirt.

"Oh, Shermie, you should have listened to me, to all of us. Now you'll pay, pay for all eternity. As we speak, the ground is accepting you, taking root in you. Soon, very soon, you will have a deep root system that will keep you alive and aware of your surroundings forever. I've made you a tree of life, something to be enjoyed for centuries and beyond. You'll never be cut down, you'll never die, and you'll give hope and happiness to all that seek shade beneath you. Children will climb your limbs, birds will nest in your branches, and lovers will carve their names in your body. And through it all you'll feel it, know it, and live it."

Mel reached out and touched the arm closest to her. "I give you eternal life, Sherman. I give you the curse of eternity as you will be, for that is what it will be for you, a curse. As queen, I decree that you shall remain strong and viable. No one will hear your pleas of help, and no one will come to rescue you. You will forever remain here in this field of hope. Grow."

Sherman's legs began to twist together, widening and strengthening into a trunk. Deep, dark wood began to form, molding and shaping to his form, elongating him to stand tall. Sprouts of limbs and branches began to erupt from his torso and arms. As long, curving wood pulled and reached for the moon that was once arms and fingers of the man, Mel asked for rain and water to fortify the new growth. Leaves began to open and unfurl as they watched, filling the branches with the greenery that would forever be there. Sherman's face watched the women. Hatred could be seen in his eyes as he developed and grew. As the wood closed around him, his eyes remained uncovered, glassed over now so he could see out, but none could see in.

When he was finished with the transformation, each woman touched the tree and gave it their mark, the mark of power and love. The mark of their kind.

The sudden gun at her head startled Pete and she looked at the women before her. Ares. They had forgotten about Ares.

"Thank you so much for the display of power, ladies, but I think I have what I've come for. Move over there, bitches, and if you make any sudden moves, I'll kill her. I do want to thank you for taking them out for me, Dilly. I wondered how I'd do it and get rid of the bodies, too. Nice trick there, sis. You'll have to teach that one to me before you die."

Pete could feel Dominic coming toward her. He was weak and she knew that if had to fight Ares, then he would die. Dominic would die. Pete did the only thing she could think of and reached for his master and friend.

"Aaron, are you close enough to save the day?" Pete knew that Aaron was close. He would not leave his mate out here without being close enough to watch over her.

"Yes, and I plan to make a grand entrance too. I do hope you know, young lady, that I am not the least bit happy with you right now. And as soon as I can, I'm going to make sure that Dominic is well aware of my displeasure with you."

Pete was not afraid. She could hear the humor in his voice. Besides, she had decided that she quite enjoyed the way Dominic showed her who was boss.

"Nag, nag, nag. I wish you would talk less and help more, you overgrown mosquito. Do you think you could maybe get your ass in gear? I'm drained and Dominic is coming. I don't think he has the strength to fight this piece of shit."

The man holding Pete was suddenly gone, lifted up into the air and then dropped as just as quickly, his head to the left and his body thrown off to the right. Aaron had torn his head from his body so quickly that Ares had not known what hit him.

CHAPTER TWENTY-TWO

"I don't care. He's been out for three days. If he doesn't wake soon, I'm going to hurt someone, and you and that...that master are going to be the first." Pete had been all right the first day, a little antsy the second, but now, three days without Dominic ever moving was starting to scare her a bit.

"Pete, honey—" Bradley started.

"Don't you dare 'honey' me again, you sadistic bastard! I think you are enjoying this. Even you were up the next day. Please, you have to make him wake up. I need him." Her voice had started to break, and she couldn't help it. He was her whole life. She needed him to yell at her, or anything, just wake up.

While she had been dealing with her brothers and mother, the men had burrowed their fingers and toes into the soft earth as she had instructed them to. Bradley felt the healing power from Shade much faster as he had not been as weak as Dominic, who had fought against the silver. Also, the men had lost a great deal of blood in the process. Dominic also had not fed recently, which contributed to his weakened state as well. When he'd tried to come to her rescue, which was a feat of great strength and love, he should have been too weak to even move, much less try to kill a man.

Bradley had been taken away by his brother, David, and the pack as soon as Bradley had been able to contact them mentally. He was in poor shape, but once the silver was removed from his skin and he shifted, he started healing immediately. He had slept through the rest of the night and most of the next day. Once he woke up, he was able to regain much strength by eating a raw steak, drinking a few beers and lazing around the pack house for the last day and a half. He was still sore and there were a couple of raw places on his back, but he was otherwise doing just fine. Unless Pete tore into him for not helping her with Dominic

Dominic had dropped to the ground as soon as Aaron stepped in front of him. Dominic had landed hard on the ground, hitting his head on a rock as he went. His body had suffered a great deal of damage and with the loss of blood; he had weakened to the point of near death. His already drained body had simply shut down, as it did when a vampire needed to heal itself and recharge. And that was how he had been since.

He had been moved to his lair when they had arrived and Doctor Reilly had been called in to examine him. He had told Pete that he would be fine in a couple of days, but to Aaron, he had told a different story.

"He's very weak. But I tell you, Aaron, I don't know what affect that vine has on him and his ability to heal. I couldn't get him to drink from me, and you said that he wouldn't from you either. But I don't think that Pete can be left alone with him if, no, when he wakes, he may hurt her. His thirst will be great. He won't stop to think before he tears into her."

"He won't hurt her. But I will keep an eye on her. She is very strong willed, you know, and I think if he lives at all it will be because she told him to. And I believe he would do anything to make her happy." Aaron was sure of this because he could do no less for Sara. And now with the children, his love for her had grown exponentially.

So someone was always in the room with the two of them at all times. Bradley had even taken his turn, sitting with the young woman for several hours before she had driven him out again.

Pete was exhausted and her head hurt. She had been sitting in the chair by the bed for two nights, but could not seem to bring herself to sit in that stupid thing again. She told the "sitter," Bradley, that she was going to undress and go to bed, and unless he wanted to see her bare-assed naked, he had better find another place to go. She watched as he thought about it, but in the end, had left, telling her that he did not want to risk having Dominic draining him one night when he least expected it. She wanted to ask him if he was serious, but was too tired.

She stripped down and crawled into bed with Dominic. She didn't want to disturb him, so she moved as far to the other side of him as she could, but she did reach out with her hand and laid it gently on his arm where her sigil had marked him. She was asleep almost as soon as her head hit the pillow, exhaustion claiming her when she thought she would never sleep.

~~~

The room was black as pitch when she sat up with a scream, an orgasm ripping through her body and leaving her in a mass of sated numbness.

"Dominic?" she asked as soon as she could take a breath.

"Now who else would it be, darling? Give me another taste, love. I need to taste your rich cream again."

He was between her legs, her thighs resting on his shoulders. He bowed his head down and licked at her pussy again and again while his fingers danced inside her, building her up to a fevered pitch quickly. When he felt her close, he suckled her clit into his mouth and bit down gently, sending her over the edge again and again, screaming his name. As her heart began to slow and her body became hers again, he kissed his way up her torso and nibbled at her nipples before taking her mouth with his in a devouring kiss.

Just before he buried his cock hard into her, he nuzzled her neck, searching for and finding her rapidly beating pulse. As he slammed his cock into her heat and wetness, he bit down on her vein. Drawing quickly from her, she came again, the walls of her sheath pulling and milking his cock, driving him over the edge with her. As her essences and blood filled his mouth, he pumped into her hard and fast, needing both his release and hers to fulfill him.

He drank from her deeply once more then sealed the small wound with a lick of his tongue. He had not needed as much as Thomas had thought he would upon waking, as her power surged through her blood, feeding him in a way no other had before. He rolled to his side as he pitched forward, taking her with him to straddle his sated body.

"I love you, Dominic."

"And I love you, Piccadilly. And I always will. But there is something of a problem I have. Aaron told me that you disobeyed him. Several times, as a matter of fact. He seemed to think that you needed to be punished. He said spanking you would probably do it. What do you think? Did you disobey my master when he told you not to go out alone, and did he not tell you to stay away from those men? I believe even I told you never to be alone as well."

"And if I had not disobeyed the man, you'd be dead. He does realize that I saved you and that wolf, doesn't he?"

Dominic could smell her now, her arousal sharp and tangy in the air. He sat up and flipped her over his lap all in one movement. He traced his fingers down her spine and the vines stirred in his wake. When he got to the crack of her toned ass, he spread her cheeks wide and brushed his thumb over her little rosebud.

"I can think of all sorts of punishments for you. Disobeying my master requires a special kind of punishment, don't you think?"

"Dominic, you know that I needed to—"

His hand came down hard across her ass. It pinked up immediately. He could feel her juices as they spread on his thigh.

"I didn't say you could speak, did I? No, I didn't. You are going to be here a long, long time if you keep this up. Your best bet is to shut up and take it. It'll go so much better if you do."

His hand came down twice more, her ass bright now. Dominic was panting. His cock ached to be inside of her, buried deep within her heat. Running his fingers through her cream, he spread it up over her seam and began to work it into her bud. Pete began undulating up and down, her own panting as loud as his.

He was on fire and nearly came when the first digit of his finger worked past the tight ring and she moaned. Working more cream into her, he stretched her, in and out.

"Pete, I'm gonna fuck you here. I'm going to slide my dick deep into you here and fuck this tight hole. Then I'm going to come, fuck you and fill you. You're so tight. I ache to be inside here." He worked another finger in and moved harder, faster.

"Oh, Dominic, I want you. You have to fuck me now, please." Her voice was deep and hard, husky with her need.

He pulled his finger out and her whimper had him nearly continue, but he needed her and helped her turn around and settle on her hands and knees. As he moved up behind her, he knelt down and nipped at her ass, licking the small wound as he inserted his fingers deep in her pussy.

"You're so wet, so hot. When my cock is inside of you, it's like being dipped in lava, a tight fist of lava."

Inserting another finger, he pushed his thumb into her ass again and worked them together, in and out, in and out. He leaned over her, nipped at the dimple at the curve of her ass, and licked.

"Come for me, Pete. Come now and then I'll fuck you."

Her pussy clamped down on his fingers, her ass too. Her scream tore from her throat. Over and over she came, screaming his name.

As soon as she began to come down, he move behind her and pushed his cock head into her heat, the virginal rings squeezing him tight. He had to stop. His body wanted to slam forward, to conquer, to claim. When she began to move back, taking more of him into her, he moved with her. For every push backwards, he moved forward. They did this, slowly, over and over until, covered in sweat, he was seated deep inside of her.

"Are you all right, baby? I'll stop if you say so."

In answer, she moved back again, harder this time, slamming against him. His balls slapped against her pussy, soaking them with her arousal. Then she did something that had him sway against her. She tightened the muscles that held him in her.

His body took over and grabbing her hips, he began to surge into her, rocking hard, pulling nearly all the way out then moving back inside. He felt his balls tighten, his climax moving up his spine. He reached around her, slid his fingers through her curls, and found the swollen nub of her clit. He pressed hard with his thumb and then slid into her heat. She nearly bucked him off when she came, her body convulsing around him bringing him with her.

Dominic shot his cum into her, deep and hot. His growl was long, coming from his toes and working out of his throat. When she came again, Dominic rocked his body coming with her.

Spent, he fell forward and over her, then in the last minute, he rolled to his back, pulling her with him. Exhaustion claimed him. Grinning, he heard her snoring softly as he fell into a deep, deep sleep.

CHAPTER TWENTY-THREE

"These men are with the police department in your family's hometown. It seems your whole family has been missing for several weeks now, since we found the body of Hephaestus, actually. And they want to know if you've heard from any of them," David asked her. David had told her that someone would eventually contact her about them and it had finally happened. He was with three men, two of which she did not know, but knew they were human.

Dominic was with her, as were Aaron and Sara. David had called her earlier to let her know they would be coming by tonight just to give her a heads up.

"No, I mean, I didn't even talk to Heph before...I mean, when he was here. In fact, I'd had nothing to do with my family for many years before this."

"Yes, ma'am, we're aware of that. The town said that you'd left about eight or nine years ago. Actually, we all thought they'd...well, we thought you were dead, that them brothers of yours had killed you. It seems your family...well, they were practicing some black arts, magic I guess you'd call it. Never put much stock in it myself, but there are those who believe, I guess. Anyway, just after we were contacted by David here about that one's brother, we started keeping an eye on the place. You know, seeing if any of them showed up or not. Nothing. But we did get a tip on some missing people and how they might be out around the property. We...well, we brought out the dogs, you see, to help find...then all the FBI showed up a few days ago."

"FBI? I don't understand. Did they not file taxes or something? And what does that have to do with a missing person?" She was not fooled.

Detective Shaw was giving the appearance of a good old boy, but she knew he was far from stupid. And she believed he knew just what had happened to them, as well —well, maybe not exactly what happened, but that they were dead.

"Not person, Ms. Bartholomew, persons. The Feds were called in because of the bodies, as in plural. Some of them have been buried on that land for fifteen years. You'd have still lived there about then, wouldn't you?" Officer Bentley asked her with a sly grin.

"Are you implying that Pete had anything to do with this, Officer Bentley? Because if you are, perhaps she should get a lawyer before this goes any further." Apparently, Aaron had noticed it as well. She looked at him and smiled.

"No, he isn't. Simmer down, Jake, we're only here to ask her what she knows, not accuse her of anything. Ms. Bartholomew, maybe you could tell us what you know. It sure would be helpful to learn something more than we got right now."

"All right, but it's not Bartholomew, it's Marshall now. But call me Pete. What I know...okay, I know that I left home when I was seventeen because they had planned to breed with me. You see, my oldest brother and mother came up with this idea that having a kid with me would create this, I don't know...powerful something. I got out. I knew they were cruel and mean to others and not just people. I believe I even reported it to you, Officer Bentley. I told you that they were stealing animals and torturing them. I even told you where the animals were tossed when they finished with them. Don't you remember? You told me that boys will be boys and don't let it worry my little head about it. Now here you are today and you're telling me that you have bodies. Well, go figure. Guess they advanced to humans, huh? Still think it was a boyish prank? As for the bodies, no, I don't know anything about them. How many are there?" She hoped there were not as many as she thought there might be.

Officer Shaw looked over at Jake Bentley with so much distaste on his face that it was easy to see he was in some serious trouble when they got back to their own station.

"So far, we've uncovered three hundred and ten. Most of them are so mutilated that we may never find out who they were. We have already begun the process of identifying some of them through dental records, about two percent so far. It may be years before we have even half of them claimed by their families."

Pete felt sick. Three hundred. Three hundred people had lost their lives to them and their sickness. Dominic reached over, picked her up, sat her on his lap, and held her close. She turned her face into his chest and cried. She cried for those poor people and for the way they had suffered.

"I'm sorry, Mrs. Marshall, I truly am," Bentley said to her as he backed away. "I don't think we'll be bothering you anymore. I'd tell you I'm sorry for your loss, but I don't think that's what this is. You're lucky, damned lucky to have gotten away when you did, and you shouldn't feel the least bit sorry that you did. You have a good life here, it seems. I'd enjoy it and forget about those brothers of yours. Sad to think that your own mother would...I shudder to think what might have become of a pretty little thing like you."

They walked to the door with Aaron and Sara, leaving Pete with Dominic, who just continued to hold her until she looked up at him.

"I killed them, all of them. But I was too late, wasn't I? I should have stayed there and—"

He cut her off with his kiss. "Had you have stayed, Pete, I'd of never have met you. If you'd have stayed, they would have had to have killed you, we both know that. You're much too strong willed and stubborn to have let them do what they wanted you to do without putting up a fight. And no, love, you did not kill them. All of you did. You, Shade, Sara, and Mel, you all killed them and that's why there are only three hundred and ten and not more. You should feel proud of yourself, baby. I know I am. Now, you are going to tell me how proud you are of me, right?" She laughed as he wiggled his eyebrows at her.

"So am I," Aaron said as he and Sara returned to the living room. "You are brave and strong, and I, for one, will cherish you for the rest of my days. Without you and your help, my children would have died, my mate as well. Had you have stayed with them, Eon would have been on the streets when it was time for him to change, instead of having help and support like he has now. He would be dead, Pete. Just another statistic of the streets. You have touched the lives of so many people and made them better because of it." Aaron kissed both her cheeks and then stood before her. "But you are, by far, the most stubborn, annoying woman I have ever had the misfortune of meeting. You argue about everything and with everyone. I swear to you, if I said it was raining outside and we were both standing in it, you'd swear the sun was shining just to be obtuse."

"Oh, yeah, like you'd know what the sun shining even looked like, you bloodsucking ass. And me, stubborn! Why, I believe I saw your picture show up when I Googled the friggin' word. The caption reads, Stubborn, Blood-sucking Idiot who Doesn't Know When to Back the Fuck Off. Aaron MacManus, a man who is not only stupid, but stubborn as an ass too. I think it might even show up when you look up the words arrogant and dickhead, too! I'm pretty sure I can fix that if it's not already there. Just give me five minutes and a computer and it will say that."

"Oh, now you're just being ridiculous. I don't even think dickhead is a real word. Dickhead...do you have any idea what that word conjures up in ways of imagery? I see this..."

The door closed quietly behind Sara and Dominic as they left Pete and Aaron to their arguing. It seemed things were finally back to normal in Aaron's Kiss.

About the Author

I woke up one morning and decided to give play time to the people in my head who were keeping me awake. Little did I know that they would be so relentless and want their time right now! I wrote for the pure joy of it and to entertain my family and friends. But mostly it was to get more than an hour of sleep without a story playing out. Of course, the more I write, the more they want. So…well, as a result of sleepless days (I work through the night as a gun toting grandma – nope not a vigilantly but an armed security guard) I have lots of stories written.

Hello! My name is Kathi Barton and I'm an author. I have been married to my very best friend Sonny for at times seems several lifetimes – in a good way, honey. And together we have three wonderful children and then the ones we brought into the world - Paul and Dale Barton, Jason and Wendy Barton and Danielle and Ben Conklin. They have given us seven of the greatest treasures on Earth. They don't live at home seven days a week! No, seriously, seven grandchildren – Gavin, Spring, Ben, Trinity, Sarah, Kelly and Kian.